SEEKER'S PROMISE

SEEKER'S WORLD, BOOK FOUR

K. A. RILEY

© 2020 by K. A. Riley. Published by Travel Duck Press.

All rights reserved. No part of this publication may be reproduced, distributed, or transmitted in any form or by any means, including photocopying, recording, or other electronic or mechanical methods, without the prior written permission of the publisher, except in the case of brief quotations embodied in critical reviews and certain other non-commercial uses permitted by copyright law. For further copyright information, you may contact K. A. Riley at travelduckpress@gmail.com.

Disclaimer

This book is a work of fiction. Names and events should not be associated with living people or historical events. Any resemblance is the work of the author and is purely coincidental.

Cover Design

www.thebookbrander.com

*For my parents, who gave me the gift of a love of reading...
not to mention many, many books.*

SUMMARY

Things are not okay.

With a certain dragon missing, Vega is faced with an awful choice: Return to Fairhaven alone, or embark on a dangerous hunt in the hopes of saving Callum.

With the help of Lachlan, Niala, and Merriwether, she makes a promise that will lead her on a new quest...and this one may be her last.

The *Seeker's World* Books:

Seeker's World
Seeker's Quest
Seeker's Fate

Seeker's Promise
Seeker's Hunt
Seeker's Prophecy, Coming in early 2021

BROKEN

"It's called the Severing."

Merriwether's voice, so often animated and playful, sounded like that of an ancient, exhausted man.

I'd never seen him looking so shattered. His eyes were bloodshot, his shoulders hunched as if weakened from carrying the weight of the world.

Shaking his head slowly, he looked down at Callum, who lay on a pristine white bed in a private wing of the Academy's infirmary.

I was seated in the chair by his side, where I'd been for hours. My eyes were fixed on Callum's chest, which slowly moved up and down, scant evidence that at least there was a little life in him.

Too little.

"The *Severing*? What does that mean?" I asked, my throat parched from endless, silent sobbing. "For him? For his dragon?"

"It means Callum and his dragon have split apart, as if someone sliced clean through the bond that had held them together for so many years. The dragon—Caffall, since we can now say his name without risking further damage—has freed himself from Callum's human side. He is liberated, if you will, although that liberty comes at a cost."

"Is he dying, too?"

Merriwether shook his head. "No. In fact, he is probably flourishing in his way."

Narrowing my eyes, I looked up at my grandfather, the Academy's Headmaster.

His words were cruel. Mostly because I knew there was an awful, penetrating truth to them. I didn't want to hear that Caffall was fine. Not when Callum was so near death.

"I don't understand any of this," I croaked through weakened vocal cords.

"The simple truth is, all dragons were once connected to human counterparts," Merriwether explained with a hint of sympathy. "They are born of a certain type of person—creatures manifested first in a shifter's mind and then into reality when the time is right. Caffall was a product of Callum's thoughts, but more importantly, of his soul. Brought to life by the young man who came of age and opened his mind to the beast who'd been dormant inside him. But as you know, the dragon is very real. And now, he is learning to exist alone—and Callum is suffering for it. He's had a large piece of himself torn away with a violent force, and it has left him weakened to a nearly irreparable level."

"So what can we do?" I asked, looking over at Niala, who was standing in a far corner of the large room with Rourke, her Familiar. He was in his black panther form, his bright eyes alert as he stared at me. "How do we help Callum? Is there some healing balm or potion you can administer?"

Niala's eyes, like mine, were wet with tears, and she simply shook her head. "I can keep him alive," she said. "He's in something like an induced coma at the moment, and he can stay like this indefinitely. But I'm afraid I can't ever heal him. Not really. It's like he's had his most vital organs removed and he's living with the help of external machinery. He's on life support, and he can't wake up. Not like this."

"You're saying he'll be like this forever."

She nodded. "I'm so sorry, Vega."

I chewed my lip for a moment, unwilling to let my voice break for the thousandth time. "I don't understand. The prophecy..."

As I spoke, the words spun their way through my mind, just as they had a thousand times before:

It is said that the heir will retake the throne...but also that he will unleash chaos and devastation on this land...Towns destroyed. Countless dead. The heir, the prophecy foretells, will become a tyrant worse than any we could possibly imagine....

Unless he finds the Ulaidh—the Treasure."

"Prophecies can be interpreted in many ways," Merriwether said, pulling me out of my thoughts. "Perhaps we all had it wrong after all."

Wrong?

Anger welled inside me in a violent, threatening wave.

"Did you know?" I asked, a growl entering my tone as I shot my grandfather a look that matched my mood. "Did you know this would happen? You *always* know the future. You must have seen it coming."

"I did not," Merriwether assured me. "I knew about the Keeper of the Lyre of Adair. I knew he would challenge you—I remember what he did to your grandmother, when she recovered the Lyre herself. But I didn't know he would..." He stopped then and scratched his cheek. "...do this. Had I known, I would have discouraged you from trying to retrieve the Lyre," he added finally. "I would have tried to stop this before it ever began. I would never have wished this on either of you. It...is a cruelty beyond imagining."

I looked down at Callum again, then said, "You're right, it is. And I believe you."

If I didn't—if I'd thought for a second that my grandfather was capable of letting me walk into my own personal Hell without a second thought for how much it would hurt me—I don't think I could ever have looked him in the eye again.

I pulled Callum's hand to my lips and kissed it softly, rising to my feet. "I'm going to go find the others who were in Cornwall with us," I said. "Let them know what's going on. They need to decide if they want to go home. I suppose there's no point in their staying here."

"No, I suppose not. Though I don't expect they'll want to leave, at least, not while you're still here. Get some food. Get some rest. Your room in the tower is still free, if you want it."

I shook my head. "I'll stay in the infirmary with Callum, if it's all right. I'm sure there's a cot somewhere I could borrow."

"I'll make sure to bring you one," Niala promised.

With a nod of thanks, I left the room and headed toward the Great Hall.

The Academy's broad, bright corridors, which had once seemed so wondrous and exquisite, now felt lifeless and dull. Carved stone arches and intricate gothic ornaments, windows that seemed weathered and pristine at once. Floating lanterns dancing along the walls like some sort of faerie enchantment had lifted them into the air.

None of their magic could begin to excite me when I knew Callum was so devoid of life, or of any potential to fulfill the destiny that had been promised to him.

I trudged along until I came to the Great Hall, where I found my party—Desmond, Oleana, Meg, my most loyal fellow Seekers—stationed together at a long wooden table.

And Lachlan, who looked up at me with his kind, green eyes, a sheepish half-smile on his lips.

I knew without asking that he could feel my pain.

He may have been a Waerg, but he was sensitive. Empathetic.

He'd gone from being someone I considered my mortal enemy—a fierce, intimidating wolf shifter—to one of my best friends. And truthfully, I wasn't sure I could manage without him.

"How is he?" Meg asked as I sat down hard on one of the wooden benches.

"Not good," I said. "He's alive, but just barely. And nothing anyone does can bring him back. It's hopeless."

"Bollocks! What's that saying?" asked Desmond. "Where there's life, there's hope?"

"Tell that to Merriwether," I retorted. "He's the most stoic person I know. Never panics. Never freaks out. But right now, he looks like he's been hit by a train and is slowly bleeding to death. It's like for the first time in his life, he had no idea what was coming, and now he has no idea how to deal with what's happened. He was counting on Callum to take back the throne, but now..."

I stopped myself, fearful I'd start sobbing again.

"So what are you going to do?" Desmond asked.

I looked over at him. I wanted to glare a stern warning that he'd better not say anything insensitive.

But he looked so sad I couldn't bear to.

"I'm going to stay here as long as I need to," I told him. "I'm going to figure out how to bring him back."

"Bring him back? But you just said—"

"Where there's life, there's hope, right?" I muttered. "I can't leave. What's the point in going back home, knowing he's suffering?" I looked around the table, set my jaw, and said, "I won't blame you guys if you go, though. I know you must be eager to see your families."

"I don't want to go home," Desmond said. "My parents would just bombard me with questions about everything. Besides, what if something happens? What if Callum wakes up, or the clues to the location of the next Relic show themselves?"

"Not to mention that time won't pass in our world, not without you there," Meg added. "It's not like we'll accomplish anything there anyhow."

"She's right," said Olly. "We'll stay in the Otherwhere until you decide to go home. We'll be here for you. For Callum."

"Thank you so much," I gushed, fighting back tears and pushing myself to my feet. I looked at Lachlan. "You can go back to Fairhaven, you know. I won't hold it against you."

"I know. But I'm not going anywhere."

"Liv will miss you."

"She won't even know I'm gone. Like Oleana said, by the time you and I return to Fairhaven, only two seconds will have passed in our world. Maybe even less. Time waits for Seekers, if they *will* it to wait, so like I said, I'm not going anywhere."

"I don't have the energy to 'will' much of anything," I sighed. "And if things go badly—if time jumps ahead like it did last time I went back—we could both get expelled from Plymouth High for disappearing for weeks."

"I don't think that's going to happen."

"No," I replied. "I guess I don't think so, either." A thought struck me. "Well, if you really do want to stay here, why don't you sleep in Callum's old room in the tower? It's not like he'll be needing it. I can show you the way."

"Sure," Lachlan said, rising to his feet to join me. "Sounds good."

We said goodbye to the others and exchanged a round of hugs before leaving them in the Great Hall.

"I'll walk you up to your room," I told Lachlan, beginning the long hike to the tower where Callum and I had slept for many nights during my weeks of Seeker training. "Then I'll be going back to spend the night in the infirmary room."

"Do you want company?" Lachlan asked as we wandered by two Zerkers who were eyeing us with a combination of hatred and pity. The Academy's red-uniformed combat specialists had always despised me for being one of the privileged Seekers who waltzed in, trained for a few weeks, then took off.

And no doubt they hated Lachlan just for being a Waerg.

"No," I replied. "Thank you, though. Honestly, I'm so tired of crying in front of everyone." I let out a bitter chuckle. "You know, sometimes I wish all those fairy tales were true. The ones about how a single kiss can raise someone from a coma. It would solve all my problems right about now."

"I know. I wish for your sake that they were true, too. But there may be another way, Vega. It feels like there *must* be."

"Do you have a theory?" I asked, immediately warning myself not to let even the vaguest hope gestate inside my mind.

"Not really. It's just—if my wolf were taken from me…if something happened to sever our connection…"

"Yes?"

"I'd want you to be the one who tried to bring him back to me. Just as I have a feeling you're the one who's going to figure out a way to bring Callum and his dragon back together."

For whatever reason, those words broke me.

A renewed flow of tears streamed down my face. My shoulders shook, and my chin quivered with the sobs I was trying in vain to suppress.

I stopped walking and grabbed Lachlan by the arm.

"What if I'm not?" I managed to mutter. "What if I can't do it?"

But Lachlan didn't reply. Instead, he put his arms around me and held onto me until I had no tears left.

PROMISE

When I'd left Lachlan to settle in Callum's old room, I made my way down to the infirmary, only to find Merriwether sitting by the bed once again.

I pulled a chair up and sat down next to him, watching the peaceful rise and fall of Callum's chest.

"He looks like he's sleeping," I said. "Like he did every night in Fairhaven, in the hours when the dragon left him alone. It's as if he's at peace."

"He *is* at peace," Merriwether assured me. "He's in no pain. That's the good news."

"Yes," I said. "I guess it is."

Reaching out, I took hold of Callum's hand. So strange to feel his skin so cold, like all the fire had left him when Caffall had flown away.

"Where do you think he is?" I asked.

"The dragon?"

"Yes."

"Why do you ask?"

I glanced over to see my grandfather looking at me sideways.

For the first time since we'd brought Callum back to the Academy, there was a distinct twinkle in his eye.

"Because of something Lachlan said. I...I think I need to go out into the Otherwhere. To find Caffall."

"Oh, you do, do you? You're simply going to have words with the golden dragon, and hope he comes back? And what makes you think he's even here, in the Otherwhere? The last time you saw him was in the sky over Cornwall."

"I can't quite explain," I said. "I can just...feel it. I think he came through when we did, somehow. Like he's still attached enough to Callum that they have to be in the same world."

Merriwether seemed to contemplate that for a moment. "So, your plan is simply to find him, and then hope for the best."

"You think it's a stupid thought."

The smile left Merriwether's eyes and he shook his head. "No. I don't. Not at all." He pushed out a breath. "Your Callum is one of the strongest, toughest, most resilient people I've met in my life. As are you. And if anyone can solve this puzzle, it's you. There may be a way to piece him back together. I'm afraid, however, that I don't know what it is."

"Neither do I. But I need to try and figure it out, and if I stay here, I'll go insane."

He rose to his feet and laid a hand on my shoulder. "If you must go, you should head toward the Northwest of the Otherwhere. If your instincts are correct about Caffall having returned to this land, the dragon is most likely concealed in the lands beyond the mountains."

"The mountains?" I asked. "I went to see them with Callum once. We were in the peaks called the Five Sisters. I could just open a Breach and get there quickly. I could..."

Merriwether closed his eyes for a moment, holding his hand up to keep me from saying anything more.

After a few seconds of silent thought, he said, "Don't go through a

Breach. Trust me on this. There will be hostile eyes turned your way, Vega, and your use of magic will make you all the easier to locate. You need to keep your journey quiet and keep your intentions hidden from the Usurper Queen. And from the wizard Marauth."

"Marauth. The one who betrayed your Order?"

Merriwether nodded. "He is bitter since his failure to obtain the Lyre of Adair—thanks to you and Callum—and he seeks ways to gain the upper hand. He will be watching for your next move, as will his servants, who live among the woods as well as the towns. You must take Lachlan with you."

When I looked like I was about to protest, he stopped me.

"A Waerg is the best weapon you could ask for. Your journey will be long, but I will supply you with horses, food, and clothing."

"Won't it take us days to get to the Northwest?" I moaned. "Even with horses?"

"It will. But it's best that you travel across land, for many reasons. This isn't a quest that can end in failure. So keep yourself hidden, as I said. Rely on Lachlan, and on any allies you meet along the way. There will be a few of them where you least expect them."

"What about the next Relic?" I asked, suddenly remembering my duty to the Academy. "There's still the Orb of Kilarin to find…and the other one…" As I spoke, it occurred to me that the nature of the fourth Relic remained a mystery.

"The remaining Relics will show themselves in due course," Merriwether assured me. "And don't forget—they tend to find their way to you, rather than the other way around. But for now, you have a more important task to focus on. Without our future leader, we will be at a great disadvantage."

"You're right," I said, glancing back down at Callum. "I need to focus all my energy on finding a way to help him. I'll talk to Lachlan first thing tomorrow morning—he's staying in Callum's old room."

"Good. I'm sure he'll be only too eager to help." Merriwether cocked his head and smirked. "The Waerg has been a good friend to you, hasn't he?"

"A great friend."

"I hope he continues to be. But be mindful of his heart, Vega."

I narrowed my eyes into an apprehensive wince. "What do you mean, his heart?"

"I think you know what I mean." With that, Merriwether smiled. "I expect it's going to be difficult in more ways than one, this journey of yours."

"If you're implying what I think you're implying, don't worry about it. Lachlan and Liv are dating. I mean, sort of. Okay, maybe only in Liv's mind. But still…"

"Still," Merriwether replied with a grin and a raised eyebrow. "Just be careful, and be kind. A Waerg who bonds with a human is a loyal companion. One who would gladly give his life for yours. Lachlan has been your guardian for a long time. He cares about you."

"I care about him, too. But I promise I won't say or do anything foolish."

My grandfather chuckled. "You've made that promise before, granddaughter of mine."

Just then, Niala arrived, wheeling a sizable and comfortable-looking cot into the room. She positioned it next to Callum's bed and draped a wool blanket over its length.

I thanked her and watched her leave with Merriwether and Rourke by her side.

Something told me I wouldn't be needing the cot after all.

With the door swinging shut behind them, I pulled myself into bed next to Callum, wrapped an arm around him, and laid my head on his chest.

I could feel the rhythmic beating of his heart. The slow pulse of his breath. But his hand didn't reach up to stroke my cheek or play with my hair. He didn't hold me.

He was a mere sculpture. An inaccessible replica of his former self. Cold and hard as marble.

There may have been breath in him, but there was no life.

"You promised you'd always find your way back to me," I whispered against his chest. "But I promise you this: I'm going to bring you back to me—no matter what it takes."

HORSES

I WOKE to hear a familiar voice breathing my name into my ear.

"Vega."

My eyelids felt as if they weighed fifty pounds, but I managed to force them open, only to realize my head was still pressed to Callum's chest. My neck was stiff from the all-night contortion as I pulled up to see who'd spoken.

"Vega—I'm so sorry, but I need you to move," Niala said when my eyes met hers.

"Yes, of course," I said groggily, forcing myself up to a sitting position. "Sorry."

I pulled myself off the bed and patted down the creases in my clothing as Rourke treaded over and nuzzled my hand with his nose. He was in his black Husky form, his eyes peering up at me as if trying to assess my current state of mind.

"You look better," Niala told me as she leaned over Callum to check his breathing.

"I *feel* a little better. I feel…hopeful. Even though I may regret saying it."

"Really?" she asked, pulling her head up to look at me. "Did something happen?"

"Not exactly. But I have a goal in mind now. A mission. Something I need to at least try, to see if Callum has a shot at recovery."

Niala clicked her tongue against her teeth. "Vega…I told you that shifters don't 'recover' from an incident like this. It's not like getting a cold."

"I know, I know. Just bear with me, okay? If it doesn't work—if I fail and fall on my face, at least I'll have tried. I can't just sit here and do nothing. Otherwise, he and I may as well both be dead."

Niala let out a long sigh that told me my hope wasn't exactly infectious. "I just don't want to see you hurt even more. Whatever you're planning, you should know the odds are—"

"I don't want to know about the odds," I snapped. "I can't afford to know. All I have right now is this tiny morsel of hope that's keeping me from collapsing in a weeping mess again. So please—let me have that much."

Niala frowned, but her lips quickly curled into a smile. "Of course." She stepped over, gave me a hug, and asked, "How long will you be gone?"

"Weeks, possibly," I said. "Maybe less, if I'm really lucky. I don't know if I'll find what I'm looking for. For that matter, I don't even know *what* I'm looking for. But that's not going to keep me from looking."

"A true Seeker, to a fault."

With a weak smile, I leaned down and kissed Callum's forehead, stroking his hair away from his face. "I'll be back once I've found Caffall," I whispered in his ear. "Remember the promise I made you, because I intend to keep it."

I LEFT Niala to look after Callum and headed to the Great Hall, where I spotted Lachlan sitting at a long table by himself. A few

Zerkers and Casters were seated around the room, eating breakfast and conversing in hushed tones while shooting quiet sideways glances at the Waerg in their midst, like they were plotting his demise.

Lachlan seemed either oblivious or indifferent to their disdain as he pulled his eyes to me and offered up a warm smile.

As I walked over to the buffet table to grab a plateful of scrambled eggs and toast, I thought of what Merriwether had told me about Lachlan having feelings for me beyond friendship. I could only hope he was wrong, particularly in light of the journey we were—possibly—about to undertake together.

The last thing I needed was for things to get awkward as well as dangerous.

"Hey," I said as I sat down with him.

"Hey," he replied. "You okay?"

"Fine," I said, taking a much-needed bite of crisp toast. "I slept, which is something."

"Good. I was worried about you."

At that, I tightened.

"You shouldn't worry," I said. "Especially about me. You should think about other things…like Liv. Don't you miss her just a little bit?"

Lachlan let out a little laugh. "Liv is at home in Fairhaven, and she's probably completely fine. I'm sure I don't need to worry about her."

"She likes you. You *should* be thinking about her welfare, not mine. I can look after myself—I don't need you to be all thoughtful and kind and frankly…weird."

Lachlan's brow furrowed. "Okay, I don't think I'm the one who's being weird right now. Where's this coming from, Vega?"

As his green eyes bored into me, I pulled my gaze down to my plate and moved my breakfast around with my fork. "You're right. Forget I said anything. I'm just a little stressed out."

"Fair enough."

We went silent for a few minutes before I finally summoned enough confidence to add, "Listen, I need a favor. A pretty huge one, actually."

"I'm here to help. You know that."

I drew my eyes back to his. "It's not just help."

"All right. Just tell me what it is, and I'll see to it that you have it."

There he was. Being noble and kind and warm again.

I wanted to slap him.

I shook my head. "You know what? I shouldn't ask. You should probably just go back to Fairhaven."

Lachlan reached out and grabbed my wrist, and I sealed my eyes shut, telling myself to hate his persistence, his protectiveness.

But the truth was, I appreciated it.

Even if I *did* want to hit him.

"Vega," he said softly. "Come on. You know I want to help."

"I want to find Callum's dragon," I said, my eyes still shut. "I need to find Caffall. And I want you to come with me."

I forced myself to look at him again, wincing in anticipation of his rejection.

Or worse…his acceptance.

Lachlan pulled back, his expression serious, though there was a strange glint in his eye. "Of course I'll come," he said cheerfully. "When do we leave?"

"As soon as we can get enough supplies together for a long trip, I guess?"

"Let's go, then," he said, pushing himself to his feet and picking up his dishes. "I'm in the mood for a perilous adventure."

WITHIN MINUTES, I found myself standing with Merriwether and Lachlan in the Academy's stables. Men and women, dressed in the Academy's linen servants' gear, were wandering in and out, carrying packages of food and piles of clothing, camping gear, and other items, which they packed in large bags already attached to a pair of worn leather saddles. As we watched, they strapped them to the backs of a couple of massive horses, one of whom was a stunning, glistening black gelding with a thick, arching neck. His long mane flowed in crimped waves, rendering him extra-exquisite.

The other horse was a chestnut with a shaggy mane that shot up in every direction and looked like it belonged on a sheepdog rather than on a noble steed.

The chestnut was a few inches shorter than his black counterpart. He was stocky, and had a white blaze running the length of his face. He was cute—if a horse could in fact be cute. But he didn't exactly look like he was up for a cross-country trek.

"Have you ridden before?" Merriwether asked me.

"When I was a kid," I said. "I took lessons here and there, and went to riding camp a few times with Liv. I can at least say I know how to pick a horse's hooves and tack them up."

"Good. And you, Lachlan?"

"I've ridden exactly once," he said. "And I wasn't very good. Waergs don't spend a lot of time around horses. We tend to make them a little…nervous."

As if to confirm the statement, the chestnut let out a snort and stomped a hoof on the cobblestone floor.

"In that case, Vega will ride Phair—he's the black one—and you'll have Dudley."

"Seriously?" I laughed. "Dudley?"

"Dudley the horse," Merriwether confirmed.

"He sounds…extremely tame. Like, pathologically."

"He is, usually. Which is exactly what you want in this

circumstance. Phair can be a little spirited, but something tells me you'll get along just fine. You've been on a dragon's back, after all."

My heart ached a little at the memory. That dragon had been a part of Callum. And now…he wasn't. He was a separate creature, probably flying somewhere over the Otherwhere. Wild and unrestrained.

Merriwether moved aside as the stable hands added a few final items to the saddlebags. He gestured to us to follow him into a small tack room, where two long, dark cloaks were hanging on hooks.

"Each of you will wear one," he told us. "They appear black in here, but they alter as you move, providing a little cover from watchful eyes."

I pulled one of the cloaks off the hook and put it on, holding my arm up only to see that it was taking on the various shades of the cobbled floor below. "It's like an Aegis Cat," I said. "It's a natural camouflage?"

"Yes, something like that," Merriwether agreed. "You'll be glad you have them. I know you can summon your Shadow form, Vega, but—and I can't stress this enough—you need to keep your magic use to a minimum until after you've found what you're looking for. Revealing your identity and your location too soon could have disastrous consequences."

Lachlan pulled on his cloak as well, and I noticed for the first time that the garment was cut up the back in order to cover a rider's legs entirely while still fitting tidily around the saddle.

As I stared at the design, two internal tendrils of fabric from my own robe wrapped themselves around my calves, securing the garment in place so that it wouldn't billow away from me as I rode.

"Genius clothing," I said to myself. "At least we have something going for us."

"Head due west," Merriwether said as we walked back out toward the horses, who were waiting, agitated, to get moving. "Watch the skies for enemies, as well as for friends. Keep your hoods up when you can. When you get to the mountains, the horses will likely tell you they've gone far enough. You can release them—they know how to get home again. Unless you find some other transportation, you'll need to go on foot from there. There is gear in your bags—blankets, food, matches, and more. Be careful, though. Since you don't yet know your exact destination, you can't know exactly how long your mission will take. So use your supplies as sparingly as possible."

He turned to a hook on one of the stall doors and pulled off a bow and quiver. Handing them to me, he said, "You'll want these for emergencies."

I lowered my chin. "Have you ever seen me try to shoot arrows? I'm horrible at it."

"Nevertheless, you may be grateful you have them."

I shook my head and gestured to Murphy, the trusty silver dagger sheathed at my waist. "I'm better at stabbing than shooting. But the thing I like best is *hiding*."

"You'll make a fine rogue yet," Merriwether chuckled, hanging the bow up once again in a gesture of surrender. "Fine, then. Just stay out of sight when you can. The robe will hide you from human eyes when you wish it to, but it will not conceal your scent from Waergs." He helped me to leap onto Phair's back then turned to Lachlan, who slipped easily up onto Dudley's saddle.

"Look after her," Merriwether said. "She's of great value to me."

"I'll protect her with my life. You know that."

"Yes. I do believe you will."

With that, Merriwether gave Phair a quick pat on the neck. "I'm sorry I can't go with you. But I want to be here, in case…"

"In case anything changes with Callum," I said with the sick realization that he wasn't entirely confident Callum would survive until our return.

"Yes. In case there's a change."

"We'll move as fast as we can," I assured him. "I still wish I could just open a Breach..."

"I know you do. Just trust me on this. And try not to worry about Callum. He's in extremely good hands." He let out a final, tired breath, and added, "I can't see your path, at least not entirely. But I have seen enough to believe you need to put yourselves among the Otherwhere's residents in order to find your way. You may need the help of those who seem hostile to your cause—but be mindful. There are many enemies out there, and at times it will be hard to tell friend from foe. Follow your instincts as best you can."

"I—*we*—will."

"Now go. The sooner you find some answers, the sooner you can come back to us."

He helped to adjust my stirrups, and I watched as Lachlan made an amusingly clumsy attempt to do the same, nearly pulling his horse's saddle sideways in the process.

"I should just run in my wolf form," he said with a frustrated huff when he'd finally settled in his saddle again. "I'm not meant to be on a horse's back."

"Something tells me you'll pick riding up very quickly," I assured him. "And we can't have you exhausted during this mission. Merriwether's right. This is the best way to go. Besides, we're going to need the supplies in your saddle bags. You can't leave Dudley here unless you plan on carrying them yourself."

"I'm sure this horse would be only too happy to stay behind," he said, taking the reins in hand, a move that Dudley greeted with an angry buck.

"Honestly, I'm glad to discover he's smart enough to be wary of wolves," I laughed. "Just...I don't know...give him a carrot and he'll be your friend forever."

"I don't have any carrots. I'll just recite romantic poetry into his ear and hope for the best."

"Whatever works, Lachlan."

Dudley let out a shuddering sigh as if he'd surrendered at last, and with a final wave to Merriwether, we headed out the door toward the wilds of the Otherwhere.

INTO THE WOODS

I'D BEEN outside the Academy's grounds before.

My very first encounter with the Otherwhere took place in the rolling green hills of Anara, to the southwest. I'd enjoyed an all-too-brief date in the mountains with Callum.

And of course, there was the nightmarish period I'd spent imprisoned in the Usurper Queen's castle, Uldrach.

But I'd never simply walked out through the Academy's front gates and headed toward the unknown. I'd never seen the woods beyond the school's borders—at least not up close.

Lachlan and I found ourselves on a long dirt road that led downhill from the grounds high on the Otherwhere's rocky east coast toward a dark horizon below. A massive, dense forest loomed in the distance, seemingly waiting for us to reach its borders so it could lure us in and ensnare us.

The day was warm and sunny, but a cool breeze kept us from overheating as our horses trudged along, apparently in no rush to distance themselves from their comfortable home. They were probably just as apprehensive about the approaching woods as I was.

Come to think of it, I wasn't sure horses and forests were a good combination. There had to be a reason the majestic animals chose to live in large, open fields.

Probably so they could see predators coming.

Oh.

Crap.

Predators.

"What's wrong?" Lachlan asked, pulling up next to me and noting the look on my face, despite my billowing hood, which I'd pulled up to conceal most of my profile.

"Just wondering what might be waiting to tear us apart in there," I said, nodding toward the distant forest.

"Probably just some of the Otherwhere's oversized bears," Lachlan said. "Ursals, they call them. Nasty buggers with massive teeth and claws the size of butchers' knives."

"You're making that up to freak me out," I said.

"Sure. If it makes you feels better to think so."

I shot him a look to determine if he was serious and came to the conclusion that I had no idea.

"Why does everything in the Otherwhere want me dead?" I lamented, grateful at least to be on the larger of the two horses so I'd be slightly harder to get at, should something come running at us with a set of gnashing, vicious teeth.

"Not everything wants you dead. At least, not every*one*. Remember, I'm here to protect you."

"And I appreciate it," I told him. "But I've seen your wolf, and impressive though he is, he's no match for giant bears."

"Don't worry. Most of the Ursals live in the south. We won't see any on this trip...*probably.*"

"Super. You're ever so reassuring, aren't you?"

Lachlan chuckled. "You can bet we'll see some Waergs. Maybe a few Aegis Cats. Probably a bandit or two. Possibly even a Cliff Lion, though they tend to stalk their human prey so quietly that they're hard to spot."

"Why are you doing this to me?" I moaned. I felt Phair shudder under me as if he could feel my panic setting in.

"Because it's fun?" Lachlan replied with a shrug. "Oh, come on. I know how you and Liv like to tease each other."

I smiled. He wasn't wrong—Liv and I *lived* to tease one another. "Sure," I said, "but usually our gentle ribbing doesn't involve talking about all the things that will inevitably kill us."

"You two literally invented a psycho killer who lives in a shack in the woods and talked for years about how afraid you were that he was going to murder you. Which would've been a neat trick since he didn't, you know, *exist*."

"Oh. Right. I'd forgotten about that."

Lachlan let out a low, rolling laugh, and I found myself joining in.

He did have a great laugh. Full-bodied and genuine, as if he knew how to thoroughly enjoy every aspect of his life. There was nothing fake about him. He wore his emotions on his sleeve—sometimes to his detriment.

"I'm glad you're coming with me," I said, and I meant it. "If you weren't here right now, I'd probably turn around and head back to the Academy."

"No, you wouldn't," he said softly as the horses' hooves clomped beneath us. "I know you, Vega."

"You're right. I wouldn't. Now let's move a little faster, shall we?"

My horse, Phair, turned out to be a smooth ride, even when we were trotting—a gait I'd always found nauseatingly bouncy when I'd taken lessons. His trot was fluid, somehow, and he moved under me as if he prioritized my own comfort over his own. I sensed his power as he strode confidently down the road, and his potential for speed, should we need it.

But I found myself hoping I'd never have to ask him to gallop at full speed.

Dudley, meanwhile, was excitable and skittish, and often

balked at the slightest wave of the grass or at a bird flying overhead. He was comically alert, his ears constantly on the move like two hyperactive satellite dishes searching for a signal.

"I don't know what's going to happen once we get in there, let alone which way to go," I confessed as we approached the woods. "No idea what to expect."

"I can help with that," Lachlan told me as he and Dudley trotted up next to me. "I've been through the Mordráth Wood many times."

"Is it really dangerous? Or were you just joking around earlier?"

"I wasn't joking, no. But it's certainly not the most dangerous place we'll be going. From what I understand, the Academy's Rangers have largely cleared out many of the hostile forces, so we should have a relatively easy time of it. There will be the odd pack of Waergs, of course, but if we're lucky, we won't run into any for a few hours yet."

"That's...reassuring?" I said with an unamused laugh.

"We'll be fine on the horses during daylight hours, at least. The forest is mostly inhabited by creatures who hunt by night. We won't make it to the border on the far side before tomorrow afternoon at the earliest, so we'll have to stay alert tonight."

"Are you telling me the forest is so big it'll take us two days of riding just to cut through it?"

"I am, yes," Lachlan said. "Then many more miles until we reach the mountains. I suspect it'll take us four days, at least, before we even see the foothills."

My stomach twisted into an angry knot. Four days to get to the mountains, then days after that to figure out what I was even looking for. Even if I was lucky enough to locate Caffall, it wasn't like I could just walk up to him and say, "Hey, I know you're enjoying your freedom and all, but I'd love if you came back to the Academy with me and did some miraculous, magical thing so you could re-enter Callum's body and we could all go back to the way things were."

I wasn't just looking for a dragon.

I was searching for a solution, a lifeline for Callum.

One I wasn't sure even existed.

Four days, I muttered with a shudder, recalling the poorly concealed urgency in Merriwether's voice. He didn't say as much, but I could tell he wasn't entirely sure Callum would last four *hours*.

"There are some outcroppings and caverns along the way that we can use for shelter tonight," Lachlan said. "I've slept in them before. They're relatively warm and fairly safe. We may even be able to build a fire without too much risk of being spotted. Of course, that won't be for hours yet."

"We'll both be sore by then," I sighed. "I'd forgotten how hard sitting in a saddle is on the legs. How are you feeling?"

"I'm fine for now," he assured me. "Dudley seems to have warmed to me a little, and I'm even getting used to the rocking motion."

"I would have thought you'd be a natural, what with an animal living permanently inside you."

Lachlan shook his head. "That animal and I share a mind. Old Dudley here is quite a different beast. He has his own mind. And apparently it consists mainly of a terror of leaves, grass, pebbles, and anything else that moves so much as an inch without warning. He's quite calm otherwise, though. I'm grateful, given that I have no idea what I'm doing."

"Well, the main lesson I remember from my riding camp is that you should always look where you want to go. The horse can read your mind, sort of. They sense what you're planning."

"Hmm. Can't I just program his GPS or something?"

"GPS?" I chuckled. "You really *are* a product of my world, aren't you?"

"Sort of, yeah. I mean, it's where I've spent most of my life."

"Well, screw GPS. You should go back to your Waerg roots. I need your keen wolf instincts if we're going to survive this journey of ours long enough to find what we're looking for."

"Yeah, about that—what *are* we looking for, exactly? I mean, I know it's a dragon, but he could be anywhere, right? Is there a reason we're heading west?"

"Merriwether said to look beyond the mountains, and I'm just going to assume he knows what he's talking about. He usually does—even when he doesn't—if that makes any sense."

Lachlan glanced my way, his green eyes pensive under the shadow of his hood. "You and he share a special bond, don't you?"

"We do." I considered my next words for a few seconds before adding, "He's...my grandfather."

To my surprise, Lachlan didn't respond immediately with a sharp exclamation of *What the hell did you just say?*

"That explains a lot," he finally replied. "About you. Your abilities. Your eyes."

"What about my eyes?" Infuriatingly, my cheeks heated as I asked the question.

"They're...interesting," he said. "They change color, depending on the light. They have this ring of brown around the pupil, but the rest of your irises move between bluish-green and hazel. But it's more than that. You always look like you're hiding something—like you know things other people don't. Your eyes are intelligent, and sort of stunning. And..."

"Okay, enough," I blurted out, hoping to stop him before he began to swell my head. "I get it. You've looked at my eyes."

"I'm a Waerg. We study people. It's how we figure out if they're friends or enemies."

"I'll admit that studying is not something I associate with Waergs."

"We do it quickly. Quietly. We size you up."

"Before you eat us, you mean. Like the wolf in Little Red Riding Hood."

"Not quite. I never had any intention of murdering you for sustenance, Vega. I just like figuring out what makes you tick."

"You might be pretty disappointed if you figured out I'm actually not that interesting," I replied, fixing my eyes ahead.

A couple of hundred feet from us, just before the edge of the forest, the road branched off in two possible directions.

"Thoughts?" I asked.

"The right will lead us closer to the mountains, and more quickly," Lachlan said. "But that means spending more time deep in the forest. It runs parallel with the Dolmar River for some miles until it reaches Volkston on the other side—a bit of a quirky place."

"Quirky?"

"Filled with misfits. Rejects. It's a place where the Otherwhere's residents go when nowhere else wants them. Grells, Waergs who've been expelled from their packs, you name it."

"Is it dangerous?"

"No," Lachlan said. "I mean, not unless you're a human. Oh—sorry. *You're* screwed."

I sneered at him. "Not funny."

He chuckled. "It'll be fine as long as we stick together. Anyhow, I suggest we head that way, particularly if you want to get to the mountains quickly."

I agreed, and when we came to the fork in the road, we headed right.

The sky was still cloudless and bright, but the moment we found ourselves surrounded by a dense canvas of trees, a heavy darkness began to engulf us.

As if sensing that they were no longer safe, the horses became agitated, snuffling in the air every few seconds.

"They're scared," I said, reaching down to pat Phair's neck in hopes of reassuring him. "I wonder what they're sensing."

Lachlan, too, sniffed at the air, then frowned. "It looks like the Rangers haven't cleared out all our enemies after all. There are a few hostile characters about. The good news is that they're probably not moving in large groups and may not be a threat. More likely spies, watching the road to see who passes. These woods are often crawling with those sent by the queen...or possibly someone else."

"You mean Marauth," I murmured. "The wizard who betrayed Merriwether's Order."

"Yes," Lachlan replied. "Though I don't know what sorts of spies he might send to this part of the Otherwhere. He would do well to be wary of Merriwether, though. Well, whatever the case, let's stick to the road for the time being. The Watchers are likely on the lookout for the Academy's Rangers or anyone else bearing the sigil of the Sword of Viviane. But they won't give us a second glance."

"Why not?"

"No one would suspect a Waerg like me of being affiliated with the Academy, which means you're safe. Mostly, at least."

"Good to know."

We rode on for a time in silence, the branches of the trees arching high overhead like a cathedral's vaulted ceiling. I couldn't hear a sound other than the soft percussion of the horses' hooves on the dirt road. Not a bird, not the snapping of a twig.

"It sounds like a cliché to say it's too quiet," I told Lachlan, pulling up next to him, "but it is. Where's the wildlife? Why is it so silent here?"

"The only birds who gather in these trees are the ones sent by their masters and mistresses. The last thing they want is to draw attention to themselves."

"I see," I replied, pulling my eyes up to the branches high above us, where I could just make out the silhouettes of a jet-black raven and a gray owl, their intelligent eyes fixed on my own. I yanked my hood around my face, reminding myself that it was a terrible idea to look into the eyes of my enemies. "Maybe we should talk about something else. I feel like we're going to give ourselves away."

"All right," Lachlan said, his voice cheerful and devoid of the anxiety mine held. "Name a topic."

"You're saying I can just pick one, and you'll start talking?"

"Absolutely."

"All right, then," I said, shooting one final glance toward the treetops before telling myself to focus on the road ahead. "Tell me about the Witches of the Otherwhere."

WITCHES

I wasn't sure if I only imagined Lachlan tensing a little at the mention of Witches.

"Why do you want to know about…them?" he asked, his eyes locked on the road unfolding before us.

"Merriwether mentioned something about them a while ago. I didn't even know until recently there was such a thing here. I guess I'm sort of fascinated by them."

"I've seen a few of them…from a distance. They aren't generally friendly with Waergs."

"So, what's their deal? Do they really fly around on brooms?"

Seeming to relax a little, Lachlan laughed. "They're a little different from what you might expect as someone who grew up in your world. The Witches I see depicted there are always green, with moles and warts, and hair growing out of their chins. They hover over cauldrons like they're cooking small children and cackling maniacally."

"You're saying the ones here aren't like that."

"You saw the Revelatrice—the woman who presented the Lyre of Adair at the Revelation Ball. You tell me."

"She was beautiful," I said. "Alluring. Interesting. I wanted to get to know her. I felt drawn in."

"Exactly."

"Are you telling me they suck you in, charm you, then do horrible things to you?"

Lachlan shrugged. "I've heard they're pretty seductive."

"Tell me more!" I said, excited for the first time in ages. I needed a distraction. A story. Anything to take my mind off the fact that I'd left Callum behind, when every inch of me wanted to be sitting by his side, holding his hand and waiting for a miracle.

"Right. Where to begin?" Lachlan said. "They live in Covens. Which are usually set up like small towns, scattered here and there, usually hidden away from prying eyes by magic. Only those who are invited in, they say, can ever set foot on their land. The question, of course, is whether anyone is ever allowed to leave."

I let out a shudder. "The Witches obviously use magic, then?"

"Some say they can harness the elements. Earth. Air. Water. Fire. But others say it's not like that—that they harness *nature itself*. Some control the weather. Others call down fire to serve them. Still others can manipulate the earth and trap their enemies in elaborate labyrinths, never to be seen again. I don't know if I believe any of it. But there is *one* rumor you might find interesting."

"What's that?"

"That there's a Coven here in the Otherwhere whose leader is descended from the most famous Witch of them all."

"Who? The Wicked Witch of The West?" I chuckled.

"No. More famous. More legendary. More real, in her way."

"Okay, I'm not sure my brain's equipped to decipher riddles right now. Who are you talking about?"

"Lady Morgana. The woman known as Morgan Le Fay. The infamous half-sister of King Arthur. They say the two of them shared a mother—Igraine. Morgana is said to have plotted the downfall of Arthur's kingdom, though that's debatable."

My eyes widened as I turned to Lachlan, grabbing the back of my saddle with my hand as Phair walked smoothly ahead.

So much of what I'd done and seen since discovering the Otherwhere was tied to King Arthur—the Sword of Viviane, known in my world as Excalibur. The discovery of the mysterious caves and tunnels under the castle Tintagel—I supposed it made sense that there would be links to the other people who'd affected his life, as well.

There was one thing that confused me, though.

"Morgan Le Fay was a real person?" I asked. "I always assumed she was just a myth, made up to add some color to Arthur's story."

Lachlan shook his head. "She was quite real. Legend has it that she was a master manipulator. And a great spell-caster. A very powerful, very beautiful woman who could supposedly seduce any man in order to get what she wanted from him. And out there somewhere," Lachlan said, nodding toward the distance, "is a Coven supposedly led by her descendant. She's apparently powerful and terrifying, and I'm not sure I ever want to meet her."

"Wow. That's sort of cool. Or awful. I'm not sure. I never could figure out if Morgan Le Fay was good or evil. The stories all seem to contradict each other—though usually, she does come off as pretty cruel-sounding."

"Probably because, like the rest of us, she wasn't a hundred percent one way or the other. She most likely had a good side and a bad one, just like we all do. But history is written by the victors."

"So," I said bitterly, "it's in the victors' interest to depict her as a harpy who seduces men and spits them out. Which means I guess we'll never know the truth."

"I guess not."

Lachlan pulled Dudley up and sniffed at the air. "I think we should head into the woods," he whispered. "Toward the river."

"What? Why?"

"A party's moving our way. Ten or more."

"A party of what?"

"Human men. But chances are they're not friends of ours."

I steered Phair into the woods and away from the road, aiming toward the river, and Lachlan followed. We were careful to avoid brittle branches or soft ground to avoid heading anywhere we might end up leaving a clear trail behind us.

After a time, we stopped and turned around, careful to keep our hoods over our heads. The horses huffed and stomped their feet on the earth but remained mostly quiet as we watched a silhouetted procession of figures in the distance, heading down the road in the direction we'd come from.

Some were on horseback, others on foot…and all of them were armed. Their armor was a hodgepodge of tired leather and old steel—a chest piece here, a helmet there. If they were part of an army, they were a poorly equipped one.

"Who are they?" I whispered.

"Probably mercenaries for hire," Lachlan said. "They may be making for the Academy, but most likely they'll head toward Rauthburg—a town on the coast where they can extort the citizens by offering protection from Waergs."

"They don't look like they could take on Waergs, though."

"No, they don't. But you might be surprised at how well some of these mercs can fight. They've been doing it their whole lives. It's all they know. Most are adept with ranged weapons."

I watched for another minute or so and then broke into a spasm of small shudders. "Can we go now? I'm feeling a little freaked out."

"Of course."

We turned again and walked through the woods until the rush of water met our ears. Shortly afterwards, we came out onto the bank of a wide, flowing river, where we allowed the horses a long drink before steering them west again.

"A few more miles, then we'll stop for lunch," Lachlan told me. "Are you holding up all right?"

I nodded, though the truth was that I was wishing myself back by Callum's side…and regretting the choice to venture out on this dubious quest of ours. If we'd run into those mercenaries—men who were literally trained to take on Waergs—they could have robbed us, or worse.

I wondered with a growing sense of dread how many other enemies we'd see before we reached the mountains.

AFTER TWO HOURS of mostly silent riding, we dismounted, fed the horses, and plopped down next to a narrow waterfall that burbled down from a steep drop-off high on the river's far side.

Lachlan was cutting into some fresh apples with a knife from one of the saddle bags. The Academy's people had also packed cheese and dried meats, as well as two full loaves of bread. The one thing I was confident about was that I probably wouldn't starve over the next few days.

But I remembered Merriwether's warning and made sure to take small portions…just in case.

While Lachlan and I were taking stock of the food in the packs, I noticed a pouch of gold currency, tucked into the bottom of each saddle bag. As we ate, I held one of the thick cold coins in my hand and examined it under the mottled sunlight.

"At least we're set if we do need to stay in some town or other," I said as I examined the coin.

"Yes, we are. Your grandfather gave us a lot of money."

"Maybe we should find a hotel tonight?" I asked, half-jokingly.

"We'll stay at the inn when we get to Volkston," Lachlan said. "But not before. We need to be far from the Academy before we can think about showing our faces to anyone. The farther we are, the easier it'll be to convince strangers that we're just visitors from some other part of the Otherwhere."

"What do you suppose the town's residents will think of us?" I asked him with a smile. "When they see us together, I mean?"

"They'll think some lucky Waerg has landed himself a beautiful human," he replied with a grin that looked more than a little wistful. "They'll think you're a fool for being with him."

My smile faded and I looked away. "You shouldn't say things like that."

"Like what?"

"Compliments. About my looks, or anything else. You shouldn't…be nice to me. It was better when you weren't."

"Okay. Sorry. I didn't mean anything by it."

"I know. It's just…"

I stopped myself.

The truth was, it *was* nice to receive such a compliment from a guy like Lachlan. He was kind, loyal, and intelligent. Not to mention drop-dead gorgeous. Many girls my age would have been all too delighted to hear those words from his lips.

If I'd been single, it would have been one thing.

But I wasn't. And as long as Callum had breath in him, I'd be his.

Hell, even if he disappeared, I'd still be his.

However attractive Lachlan might be.

"Vega," he said softly.

"Hmm?" I replied, pulling my eyes back to his.

"I *know* you love Callum. You don't have to worry that I'll try anything. Or that I expect anything. I can't promise I won't find you beautiful, but you have my word that I'm not here in the hopes of stealing you away from him. At least, not right now."

"You're talking like I'm property to be passed around," I retorted, irritated at his choice of words. "I'm not a thing you can steal."

"You're right. You're not. You're an impressive, independent, strong young woman. I apologize for my phrasing."

I pushed out a breath then said, "Apology accepted."

For some reason, a pang of guilt assaulted me then.

"Look, Lachlan…you're a good guy. A *great* guy. I trust you, or I wouldn't have asked you to come with me. I consider you one of my best friends." I snickered. "I mean, how crazy is that?"

"Friends," he echoed, pulling his chin down to stare at his feet. "Yep. It is crazy to think we're…*friends.*"

He said the last word like it tasted bitter on his tongue, a pill I'd forced him to swallow.

"My best friend has the hots for you," I said. "And like you pointed out, I'm in love with someone else. Maybe if circumstances were different—"

"But they're not," he said, leaping to his feet with a smile. Whatever dark mood he'd been in a few seconds earlier seemed to have faded quickly. "I'm well aware of the circumstances. And you and I have a dragon to find. So let's go do it, before one of us says something really stupid."

When we'd packed up our things once again, we mounted our horses and followed the river for several miles. By now, I was growing sore from sitting in a saddle all day, albeit grateful that our journey had remained relatively uneventful.

"In a couple of hours, we can begin looking for a place to camp," Lachlan told me as the sun began to lower beyond the trees. "We'll have to stay near the horses, of course."

"Because they could get stolen?"

"More likely eaten."

I looked over to see if he was joking.

But it seemed he was dead serious.

DUSK

"Over there," Lachlan said after we'd ridden for some time, pointing to something on the far side of the river. "Do you see the wall of stone beyond the woods?"

I looked over to see something concealed behind a dense tapestry of mature trees. After a second, I was able to make out a gray cliff face that seemed to stretch for miles in either direction. It wasn't very tall—maybe twenty or thirty feet—but it was still daunting.

"We'll go over and set up camp in one of the caverns cut into the rock," Lachlan said. "There are many to choose from."

"Sure," I replied, staring at the river. "Where's the bridge to take us across?"

"There's no bridge."

"You're serious?"

"Yes. The closest one is thirty or so miles from here."

"That means finding another way to cross the water."

"It does," Lachlan snickered.

Damn him for enjoying this.

"On our horses?" I asked with more than a hint of terror in my voice.

"You might be surprised to learn horses can swim quite well."

"But all our stuff…the food in our bags…"

"Don't worry, Vega. Just trust me."

"Everyone keeps saying that." I huffed out a defeated breath and finally nodded. "Fine. I trust you," I assured him. "But I'm not sure I trust the river."

The truth was, my mind was swimming with negative thoughts. Lachlan and I had barely spoken since our last break, and I was convinced I'd offended him with my pre-emptive and presumptuous rejection.

I felt foolish and cruel at once, and part of me wondered if his talk of fording an impossible river was some form of punishment.

Or maybe I was only imagining it out of a sense of guilt. Whether because I didn't care about him as much as he wanted me to, or because I felt like I was somehow betraying Callum by even *thinking* about my feelings for another boy, I wasn't entirely sure.

Either way, I felt wretched, and I'd begun to dread the night ahead.

With Lachlan in the lead, we rode in silence for a time, until I was able to see a carpet of smooth, flat stones lining the river's bottom, sparkling up in the waning sunlight like polished gems.

"It's shallow here," I said triumphantly. "We can walk across!"

"I *told* you to trust me," Lachlan said with a smile.

It seemed that he, at least, wasn't dwelling on our earlier conversation.

The horses stepped into the water and started out across the river, clearly nervous that the current would suddenly pick up and carry them violently to some unknown destination.

Their ears twitched and they tossed their heads, but they soldiered on over the rocky bottom of the shallow water without incident.

When we'd reached the far side, Lachlan led the way toward

the cliff face. Before too long, we found a suitable-looking outcropping that offered us shelter and protection.

"I'll need to gather some wood for a fire," Lachlan said as he dismounted and removed Dudley's bridle, leaving nothing but a light leather halter. I did the same with Phair, and we tied them loosely to a couple of nearby trees with a length of rope and enough slack to let them go foraging for grass and clover on the forest floor.

"Will you be okay alone for a few minutes?" Lachlan asked, shooting me a cryptic look before scanning the woods around us with his keen eyes.

"Sure," I replied, though I wasn't convinced I meant it. Merriwether's warning about not using my magical skills meant that even with my camouflaging cloak, I couldn't hide if someone with a keen sense of smell and very sharp teeth happened along.

But I couldn't exactly go with Lachlan—after all, someone had to stay to keep an eye on the horses.

"Just…come back soon, okay?"

"Of course," he said. "I'll be close by." Shooting me one more long, unreadable look, he disappeared into the woods.

With a nod, I hugged my arms around my shoulders and shivered. By now it must have been five o'clock or later, and dusk was threatening to bring along some frigid temperatures. For all the blankets that Merriwether's people had packed for us, I still wasn't sure I'd survive the night without coming down with a serious dose of hypothermia.

Freezing or not, I had to admit that the landscape surrounding the cliff was wild and beautiful. Across the river, a tall hill in the distance—practically a mountain—climbed to a jagged summit above the trees, and a series of similar peaks rose up beyond it as if signaling our proximity to *actual* mountains. I wondered for a moment if we were nearing the foothills of the Five Sisters, but then I remembered with a swell of disappointment that Lachlan had said it would take us four days to reach them.

Pacing the forest floor and trying my best to stay warm, I found myself musing about what the next day and our visit to Volkston would bring. It was going to be strange, to say the least, to see Grells—a sort of fur-coated human-animal hybrid—and Waergs living together in one place. I would never have guessed the two could dwell that close together without constantly trying to kill each other.

I realized with a shudder that I might find myself the only human in town.

Which meant it would be all but impossible not to draw unwanted attention.

As the grim truth set in, I became more grateful than ever to have Lachlan along for this dangerous mission. As strange and awkward as our journey had been so far, he knew the woods and the inhabitants of the Otherwhere as well as anyone. Without him, I would have been lost, both mentally and physically.

Stepping toward our shallow quasi-cave carved into the imposing cliff face, I thought about the last time I'd walked into the depths of a cavern.

It was in Cornwall, under the castle Tintagel's ruins, in the cave that had led to the moment of Callum's Severing from his dragon, Caffall.

The moment that had destroyed both of our lives.

It had happened such a short time ago. And yet I'd endured an eternity of anguish since then.

This cave, at least, was more like an overhang of rock than a dark, enclosed space with confining walls. It had a stone floor and ceiling, but its sides were mostly open to the forest, so at least there was no real danger of getting trapped inside.

That was about all it had going for it, though. Sure, we had blankets, but we'd still be sleeping on a surface of ice-cold stone.

If Callum had been with me, I would have been excited to

sleep pressed against him, both for warmth and for comfort. He'd wrap an arm around me, squeeze me to his chest and whisper welcome assurances that everything was going to be fine.

But Callum wasn't here.

And I was pretty sure I was going to spend the night trying to find excuses to stay as far away from Lachlan as I could get.

I was still plotting out our sleeping arrangements when the nearby snap of a twig startled me into instant focus.

I spun around to see that the horses were still standing by their respective trees, but their heads had shot up, their eyes and ears on high alert.

Somewhere close by, another twig snapped, then another.

It's just kindling, I told myself. *Dry twigs that Lachlan is gathering for the fire.*

"Glad you're back," I called out toward the woods with a sigh of relief. "Listen, I was just thinking we should—"

But my words were cut short when a strange man stepped out from between the trees, his bright eyes locked on mine.

INTRUDER

THE MAN HAD DARK, stringy hair and intense gray-green eyes. His skin was dirty and his torn linen clothes weren't much more than a collection of shredded rags.

He cocked his head to the side as he eyed me.

"Who are you?" I asked, my hand reaching for my dagger.

"Who are you?" the man parroted, his head bending to the other side as he sniffed at the air. "A human," he growled. "A human...in *our* woods."

"I...I'm sorry...I wasn't under the impression that anyone owned these woods," I said as respectfully as I could.

The stranger had to be a Waerg. Who else would tilt his head like a confused dog while referring to me as "human?"

Some Waergs, like Lachlan, were articulate, even eloquent. But this one was more feral than most, and exuded viciousness. He looked like he wanted to tear me limb from limb then feast on my bones.

"We own the woods," he snarled, taking a step closer. "*We* do."

"We?" I asked, my eyes darting left and right as I pushed back at the urge to pull my blade from its sheath at my waist. Maybe I could talk myself out of this situation, rather than risk a fight with such a wild creature. "Who exactly is *we*?"

"My kind," he said with a grim smile. "My...pack. The human wants to see my true form, does she?"

He stood staring at me for a moment, licked his chapped lips, then shifted into the form of a mangy-looking, thin brown wolf. His fur was matted and vile, tangled in dense nests of dried grass and other detritus.

But his eyes were bright, his teeth massive, jagged, and gleaming in the fading daylight.

Desperate now, I pulled my knife from its sheath, holding it in a shaking hand between the wolf and my vulnerable torso, and wishing I felt confident enough to summon a shield or some other barrier between us without drawing the attention of even more frightening enemies.

I was only a day's ride from the Academy. Not far enough along on our journey to risk revealing my identity.

Lachlan...where are you?

The wolf began to pace in a semi-circle in front of me, forcing me to twist around to keep my eyes locked on his. The way his tongue lolled out of his mouth convinced me that he was laughing at me, toying with my mind, and assessing me, all at once. He was studying me, as Lachlan had said.

Probably trying to figure out if he'd do better to kill me outright or just injure me, so he could go back and tell his pack about the lone human girl who was stupid enough to wander into the woods without proper protection.

It wasn't until he stopped and sniffed at the air that the Waerg seemed to notice our horses, who were now prancing frantically in place, the whites of their eyes wide and glistening in the moonlight as they stared at the creature.

Turning toward the river, the Waerg began to pad toward Phair and Dudley, who reared up in shallow leaps, letting out snorts of protest.

If the Waerg killed them, Lachlan and I would be in serious trouble—even if the intruder didn't so much as touch *us*. Without our mounts, it would take days on foot to reach the far border of the woods. Not to mention the fact that we'd be far more vulnerable to attacks.

"Hey, Wolf-man!" I shouted, hoping to draw the intruder's attention as he stalked toward the horses. "Come back this way! I'm the one you want!"

Seemingly irritated, the creature circled back toward me when he heard my voice, pressing his head low to the ground, sniffing as he advanced. But he seemed to sense a threat then, because he stiffened, raised his head, and looked around, his bony paws freezing in place.

I whipped around to see Lachlan striding toward us from between the trees, a bundle of firewood in his arms.

"You all right, Vega?" he asked, his voice full of menace as he narrowed his eyes at the Waerg.

I was sure I heard the low rumble of a growl rattling its way up his throat.

"For now," I replied.

"I'm sorry I took so long, but I'm here now."

He set the wood down and walked over to position himself between the intruder and me. Then, facing the Waerg, he spoke.

"Leave. Tell your pack not to come here tonight. If they do, you and they will all die. Do you understand me?"

The wolf growled then half-lunged at Lachlan, swatting a paw at the air between them in threat.

"Cailh phregh," Lachlan spat in a language I didn't understand, gesturing toward me with one hand. "La dara sé mien."

The wolf pulled his head up, gawked at Lachlan then at me, then turned and raced back into the woods.

"What the hell did you just say to him?" I stammered, pressing a hand to my chest and breathing heavily when I was finally confident we were alone. "I was sure he was going to try to eat my internal organs for dinner."

Lachlan turned to me, ignoring the question. "Are you all right, really?"

I nodded. "Yes, like I said. But seriously…what did you tell him?"

"Nothing."

"That wasn't nothing. You scared the hell out him. He looked like you just told him you were going to rip his head off and slurp out his brains."

"You really want to know?"

"Yes."

Lachlan locked his eyes on my own. "I told him you were mine."

NIGHT

"What the hell do you mean, I'm yours?" I snapped, anger roiling its way through my bloodstream.

Lachlan walked away from me and began to gather the wood he'd dropped earlier. "The Waerg now thinks I've claimed you. Which means he would have to fight me—on his own—and win, if he wants to take you from me."

I let out a laugh of half anger, half disbelief. "What kind of backward society are you from?" I asked. "Seriously? I told you I'm no one's property."

"It's not so simple as that," he said, heading into the shelter's opening to lay the wood down. "It's a bit of an old-fashioned mindset, I'll admit. And I don't subscribe to it. But others do, and it's a way to avoid conflict. A Waerg in search of a mate won't try and take another's away, unless he's confident in his chances of winning the fight. In a twisted way, our mangy friend was following an ancient code of honor."

"You said *mate*," I said, dropping to the ground and pulling my knees up under my chin, eyeing Lachlan with renewed scrutiny. "But you're telling me you don't buy into that kind of talk?"

"What kind of talk, exactly?"

"The notion that you can just lay claim to a human woman, whether she likes it or not."

"No! Of course I don't buy into it. That's the kind of talk of medieval men who think they can buy a woman from her father with nothing more than ten silver coins and a goat."

"But obviously, that Waerg thought I was his for the taking. He thinks women have no agency. That we're just possessions."

"Yes, but he wasn't the sharpest tool in the shed, in case you hadn't noticed. He's a Feral. He goes purely on instinct. Like any animal, his instinct tells him to hunt, mate, eat, sleep. Not necessarily in that order."

"So you're seriously telling me if you hadn't come back, he might have tried to make me his…mate?"

"No. He would more likely have killed you when you resisted him."

"Okay, then. Good to know."

Lachlan let out a laugh and finally seemed to relax, which was enough to get me laughing, too. "I'm sorry, Vega. I didn't pick up his scent when we first got here. He's a sketchy moron, but he was smart enough to stay upwind. I should have been more wary. I'm so sorry."

"It wasn't your fault that some weird prehistoric wild-man wanted to turn me into dinner, or make me the mother to his little feral cubs, or whatever."

Lachlan stepped over to sit down next to me, close enough that I could feel the heat from his body.

"It would be best not to light the fire," he said. "It might attract more of his kind."

I nodded. Under other circumstances, I might have eased away from him. But in that moment, I was grateful for his proximity and thankful to be reminded that he was as loyal a protector as I could ask for.

"I'm sorry for what I am," he told me, leaning back, his palms flat on the ground. "I'm sorry that every time you meet up with a Waerg, you're reminded that there's something repulsive under my own human façade. It's like this repetitive message that *Lachlan is fatally imperfect*. That's I'm so far from…"

He let out a sigh.

I gave him a gentle shoulder nudge in return. "I've told you before that I don't hold it against you—even if it might seem that I do. There are a lot of bad humans out there, but I wouldn't exactly love it if you called me out for *their* behavior."

"I know. But I just…I care what you think of me. When we first met—I mean, face to face on that beach in Fairhaven—I'll admit, I didn't like you much. I assumed things about you, because of what I'd heard from the other Waergs around town. Everyone said you were the Chosen One, Merriwether's star Seeker…like you'd had everything handed to you on a silver platter. They were all the things that make me judge and despise a person. But it was only because I'd let myself forget what you've gone through in your life before that. I forgot what I'd seen with my own eyes."

"My parents' deaths, you mean," I said, turning to look at him.

Lachlan nodded. "Most important, I forgot that you're good, Vega. Like, a genuinely good person. Better than anyone I know. You constantly sacrifice bits of yourself to help others—I mean, look what you're doing right now. You're hanging out in the woods, being threatened by Ferals, all in the hopes that you can find some miraculous cure for Callum's affliction. You're not selfish, like so many people—*and* Waergs—I've met in my life. I can only hope that one day I'll be half the person you are."

Overwhelmed by the praise, I turned my eyes away from his, choosing instead to take an interest in the pile of wood stacked tidily on the ground. "You're still painting way too kind a picture of me, Lachlan. You're wrong about me, you know."

"Oh? In what way?"

"I *am* selfish. So selfish. If you only knew." I closed my eyes.

"When Callum was given the test in Cornwall—when the Keeper of the Lyre asked him to say his dragon's name—I wanted him to refuse. I wanted him to come with me. I wanted us to escape, to leave that place. I knew how important the Lyre was to the Academy, to the Otherwhere, to *everyone*. But I didn't care in that moment, because I thought my happiness—*our* happiness—was all that mattered."

"So why didn't the two of you just leave?"

"Callum wouldn't have, even if he could have. He's more noble than I am. More generous. More kind—more of a leader. But in the end, we *couldn't* leave. The choice was either for him to say his name, or for us both to die, and he knew it. He gave up his life to save mine."

"You've also made difficult choices in order to save others."

"No," I said. "I've tried. But I've failed, more than once. I think I put other people—my allies, my friends—in more danger than they'd be in if I didn't exist, to be honest. Even *you* might get killed on this trip of ours. And if you do, I'll—"

I bit my lip to silence myself.

"You'll what?"

I remained silent for a few seconds before replying, "I'd never forgive myself, Lachlan. And I'd never forgive you for choosing to come with me. So the truth is, you probably should have stayed a million miles away from me."

"I couldn't stay away from you if I tried. The truth is, I'd go to the ends of the earth for you."

I blushed then, and turned away again to conceal my face from him. Despite the encroaching darkness, I was sure he could see the embarrassment painted on my cheeks.

I'd pinched myself a thousand times for having been so fortunate as to meet Callum—for how lucky I was to have ended up with him.

And now, this strange boy—the kindest, most eloquent, most

charming Waerg I'd ever met—was sitting next to me in the dark, his voice laced with quiet longing.

And I couldn't even tell him I appreciated the sentiment.

I couldn't say anything at all. Not without betraying some part of myself.

"Don't forget. I'm not here purely out of benevolence, or even out of affection for you," he told me, his voice a mere breath on the air. "I'm here because my word means something, and I believe in staying true to it. Remember, I made a promise to your mother."

Smart boy, turning the topic to my mother.

That was far more innocent, far easier to confront than our complicated feelings for each other.

"Well, once we're done with this little quest of ours, I think you can consider your debt paid," I said, managing to pull my eyes to his and smile. "You've done a lot for me. Too much, really."

For the first time, I noticed that his pupils were outlined in a fine ring of silver, threading like a sunburst toward the dominant green color of his irises. His eyes were dark and bright at once, shining like reflectors in the fading light.

They pulled me in, made me want to study him closer.

But I was afraid to.

There was something a little magical about Lachlan. More than most Waergs. There was a depth to him I had yet to figure out.

"Who were your parents?" I asked.

"My parents?"

"Yeah. You know all about mine. I want to know about yours."

He sucked on his lower lip for a second. "To be honest, I don't know anything about them."

"Wait—really? You never knew them?"

"Really. For as long as I can remember, I was a member of Maddox's pack—the pack of Waergs you met in Fairhaven."

I stiffened at the name *Maddox*. The light-haired woman who'd tormented me since my seventeenth birthday. A servant of the Usurper Queen whose sole purpose in life seemed to be to make mine miserable.

"So who looked after you?" I asked.

"I was raised by wolves, literally. But I never had a mother or a father—not in the human sense."

I reached out but stopped short of touching him. Suddenly self-conscious, I pulled my hand back and tucked it into my lap. "I'm sorry," I said. "I didn't know that about you."

"It's okay. It's not uncommon in packs like mine. We live a more communal sort of life than most humans. Honestly, I'm not even sure I want to know who my parents are. They'd probably turn out to be mass murderers or something. Most Waergs don't have the greatest track record on human rights issues."

"You don't know that. You're no cold-blooded killer. Maybe it's not in your blood—which means maybe it wasn't in theirs, either."

"Anything's possible, I suppose."

Lachlan turned to reach for his pack, which was sitting a few feet away, and pulled out some dried meat and cheese wrapped in a bit of cloth. "Hungry?" he asked, offering me some.

"Famished, now that you mention it."

We devoured a little of the food and watched as the sky changed color from dark purple to jet-black. The temperature lowered, and before long, I found myself shivering.

"Should we risk a fire?" I asked.

He shook his head. "I'm sorry. I don't want to put you in more danger."

"Okay...but I'm not sure Merriwether's thin blankets and our cloaks will be enough to keep us from freezing to death."

Lachlan smiled and took another bite of cheese. "We'll be fine," he said. "I have a fur coat, remember?"

"Okay, so you're looked after. But I forgot my mink coat at home. So what am I supposed to do?"

I looked over at him to see him throwing me the same cheeky grin I'd watched him give Liv a hundred times. Flirtatious and innocent at once. He was pure charm, and it was hard at times to resist him. And it *wasn't* hard to see why Liv was so infatuated with him.

"You really think I'm going to snuggle up to a wolf all night?" I asked with a laugh.

"You don't have to," he replied with a shrug. "But I'd definitely recommend it. We have a long journey ahead of us, and you wouldn't want to catch a nasty cold on night one."

I rolled my eyes. "You're very good at selling yourself. You know that, right? You make yourself sound so harmless, like *Don't worry, Vega. What's the worst that could happen if I spoon you all night?*" I snickered. "You really *are* the wolf from Little Red Riding Hood, aren't you?"

Lachlan held his hands up as if in surrender. "Hey, I'm *completely* harmless. To you, anyway."

"No, you're definitely not."

With another chuckle, he rose to his feet. "I'm going to take the horses down to the river for a drink. I'll be back soon. Don't get eaten by wolves in the next three minutes, okay?"

"Mm-hmm."

While he was gone, I spent my time spreading out the blankets and folding a sweater into a makeshift pillow. It wasn't exactly late, but I was exhausted all the same, and all I wanted was to find myself asleep so the next morning would come sooner.

When Lachlan returned, I was already lying down, my knees tucked up almost to my chest as I tried my best to convince myself that I wasn't freezing...despite the fact that my teeth were chattering, and I was lying on a bed of ice-cold stone.

Without a word, Lachlan skulked nearer, shifted into his dark gray wolf form, and lay down, wrapping himself around my shivering body like the warmest fur coat imaginable.

"Thank you," I whispered in the dark.

I stroked my hand over the fur on his side before pulling it back, tucking it under my chin, and closing my eyes tight.

THE GOLDEN GOOSE

When I woke up, I found myself alone in the cold dampness of our stony shelter.

My breath puffed out in a tidy white cloud as I pushed myself to my feet, pulling my thin wool blanket around my shoulders.

"Lachlan?" I called out.

My voice quivered as I tried again.

A few seconds later he came into view in the distance, leading the horses up from the river.

"Just getting ready for the day's ride," he called to me. "I'll be there in a second."

I smiled, not daring to admit how relieved I was to lay my eyes on him.

Or how guilty I felt.

I'd spent the night wrapped up in Lachlan's wolf's fur, all the while dreaming of Callum. Of his voice, his face, the touch of his fingers on my skin. Vivid memories that had awakened all my senses at once, even as I pressed against someone else for warmth.

All this is for Callum, I told myself. *The cold. The danger. The risks we're both taking. All so I can find a way to get him back, so we can be together again.*

No. I didn't have the time or the energy for guilt. If Lachlan could keep me alive long enough to succeed at whatever mysterious miracle it was I was hoping to pull off, then so be it.

Callum would understand.

And maybe I'd even learn to forgive myself.

When he came up from the river, Lachlan was smiling and practically glowing with energy.

I wasn't sure if it had anything to do with the previous night's quasi-intimacy, or if it was merely that he'd woken up refreshed after a sound sleep. Either way, I was grateful that he didn't mention our sleeping arrangement…or any of our awkward topics of conversation from the previous day.

"You ready for another long ride?" he asked as we put the bridles on the horses.

"I'm not sure I have a choice," I said, patting Phair's thick, glossy neck. "But yeah, I think I'm good to go."

After a quick bite of leftover cheese and bread, we mounted up and headed west, making our way toward Volkston, the town Lachlan had told me about. The sky was clear and the air fresh, and I was even beginning to feel hopeful.

During the next few hours of the mercifully peaceful journey, we passed the time chatting about everything from our favorite foods to memories from our childhoods. Though I was sore from the previous day's ride, the aches dissipated with time, and we seemed to be moving at a good, fast clip.

Or maybe it was just the fact that we had a destination in mind that made me feel we were accomplishing something. Lachlan assured me several times that we'd make our way out of the woods before sundown.

After several hours during which we only stopped twice to let the horses rest, I finally spotted something in the distance.

"I see smoke," I said, pointing. "There, above the trees."

"From the chimneys," Lachlan said, his bright eyes fixed on the distant plumes. "That's Volkston. It's still a few miles off, but we should be there within the hour."

I nodded, excited that the next stop on our journey was in sight.

An hour or so later, though, my confidence began to wane.

As we emerged from the woods, the town spread itself out before us. Under the bright, cheery sky was a depressing array of what looked like tobacco-colored houses. Some were made of ancient, weathered wood. Others were coated in stucco that had probably once been white, but was now a sort of mustard-yellow, stained from mud, smoke residue, and who knew what else.

I pulled my hood low over my face and followed Lachlan, who steered Dudley down the main street and through a marketplace populated by shifty-eyed figures who had the characteristics of both human and animal. Some reminded me of Kohrin Icewalker, the Grell I'd met in the mountains on my date with Callum.

Half mountain goat and half man, Kohrin was an unusual-looking creature, but appealing, as well. He was polite, friendly, and intelligent.

Most of Volkston's inhabitants, on the other hand, had a feral quality like the Waerg I'd encountered the previous evening in the woods. The locals looked as if they were hunting for their next meal among the crowd.

Though I found them daunting, I couldn't deny that they were intriguing, as well. Bright-eyed and wily-looking, some had the fur-coated limbs of large cats, their long fingers accented by long, pointed claws. Others had hooves at the ends of their their backward-bending legs.

I reminded myself that I was the anomaly here. I was the intruder, the foreigner, the one deserving of wary looks.

As Lachlan and I advanced, a quiet hostility lingered on the air around us—not so much directed our way as at the world in general.

"Where exactly are we going?" I asked when I was close enough that he could hear me.

"The Golden Goose," he replied. "At the far end of town. It's an inn run by an old friend. They'll look after the horses and feed us well, if we ask them to. Just don't make eye contact with anyone between here and there, if you can help it."

"Okay," I replied, dodging my way around a Grell who was pulling a cart filled with vegetables. He shot me a curious grimace that reminded me to avert my eyes. "I'm not sure it matters—I feel like everyone here can smell exactly who and what I am."

"We'll be there in just a few more minutes. Try not to worry too much. You may be a curiosity, but most of Volkston's residents keep to themselves and don't want to cause problems. There's enough tension in this place as it is."

"You said *most*," I repeated. "But it's the exceptions to the rule I'm worried about."

When we finally pulled up in front of the inn, I relaxed my shoulders, which had been locked in a state of high tension since we'd stepped into town. Forcing myself to breathe, I dismounted, scanning the area behind us for any curious observers, but saw nothing except the town's grumpy-looking population going about its business.

"You're right in thinking they don't care much for visitors," Lachlan said. "Particularly not human ones. But the good news for us is, the last thing the town wants is to start a war. These Waergs and Grells came here to escape humans, not to get into fights with them."

"I *guess* that's good news," I said, just as a squat figure stepped out from a dark, arched laneway to one side of the inn. He was hunched over, his face covered in a thick layer of brown fur. With his tangerine-colored eyes, he reminded me of a stray cat who'd hung around our neighborhood in Fairhaven when I was little. I remembered him going from door to door each evening, mewling for scraps. He'd broken one of his hind legs at some point, and like the creature in front of me, he'd always walked with an awkward gait...though at least he never seemed to be in pain.

"Take your horses for ya?" the man asked. "I'll put 'em in the stable, groom 'em, and feed 'em."

Lachlan gave me a reassuring nod. "Thank you," I said. "That would be great. And we'll make sure to make sure you're well compensated for your troubles."

"Thank you kindly, Miss," the man said before taking each horse by the reins and leading them back down the alley.

"He's half puma, that one," Lachlan said, watching him go.

"Why's he so bent over?"

"Some Grells' skeletons develop in a streamlined way, and result in graceful movement and elegant posture. Their human and animal sides meld into something perfectly functional—something better than either human or animal. But some aren't so fortunate. It's like their human and animal halves fight one another while they're trying to decide which is their dominant side, and the battle is never quite resolved. From the looks of our stable-hand friend there, the cat inside him tried to win out but lost."

"Poor guy. It can't be comfortable for him."

"No, I don't imagine it is. Come on, let's head inside," Lachlan said with a last look of sympathy at the entrance to the alley. "But do yourself a favor—don't ever let a Grell hear you calling them 'poor' anything. Not every creature is meant to be human, you know. Just because you walk upright and have less fur doesn't make you the physical ideal in this world."

I blushed, bit my lip, and nodded my understanding. He was right—it was arrogant to assume that anyone should want to look or walk like I did. I was the least special creature in this entire town, after all. I lacked the Grells' or Waergs' senses, their instincts, their abilities. I was inferior in almost every conceivable way. "I didn't mean anything by it," I moaned.

"I know, Vega," Lachlan replied, reaching a reassuring hand out, which I gratefully took. He gave it a reassuring squeeze before letting it go again.

He led me inside, where a small pub awaited us, much like the one at our inn in Pevethy, in Cornwall. It was warm and inviting, its walls and ceiling lined with weathered wood beams that looked like they'd just barely survived several wars. Some were blackened here and there with scorch marks. Others looked like they'd been hacked with hatchets or with the swords of drunken fighters.

Lachlan and I sat down at the bar, placing our packs on the floor between us, and I found myself pressing close to him for comfort.

"Two ales," he told the bartender—a man with light hair and eyes, and skin close to the mocha shade of my own.

The bartender gave me a side-eyed look, a half-smile on his lips.

"Where you two coming from, then?" he asked as he poured our drinks.

I opened my mouth to reply, but Lachlan laid a quick hand on top of mine. "Kaer Penthal."

"Penthal, eh? You've ridden a long way," our impressed bartender replied. "What brings you to Volkston?"

"Family. My aunt lives close by, in a cabin in the hills. She's taken ill, and we thought we should come see her in case the worst should happen in the near future."

As Lachlan spoke, his accent, which had never quite sounded like that of anyone from my world, thickened and evolved.

"Ah. Your aunt." The man shot me another look. "But *you* ain't from anywhere near Kaer Penthal, Missy," he said, sniffing the air in a way that made my skin crawl. "Are ya?"

"She's with me," Lachlan said, gripping my hand as if to tell me not to answer. "In case you're getting any ideas. And the Goose's owner is an old friend of mine, so I'd suggest you take your eyes off her if you want to remain employed by this establishment."

The bartender shifted his eyes to Lachlan's before pulling his chin down in what looked like an act of submission. "My apologies, Sir," he said. "I didn't realize you were friends of Sindor's. Ale's on me, then."

He stepped away to tend to another customer, and I threw Lachlan a look. "What's his deal?" I asked. "Oh, God. Is he another Waerg?"

"He is. And he was a little too interested in you for my liking. Are you all right?"

"Of course I am. But I'm still not used to being eyed like that. It was…intrusive."

"It's the unfortunate price of being a Gorge," Lachlan said before taking a sip of his drink.

"A what?"

"A Gorge. It's a word Waergs use for a person whose scent drives them mad."

"You didn't mention this last night when that Waerg in the woods was acting all weird."

"That's because you were already freaked out enough by the mere fact that he was eyeing you as a potential mate. I didn't want to throw any more creep factor at you."

"Are you saying my scent drives *you* mad, too?" I asked, taking firm hold of the stein in front of me.

"Do you really want to know?"

I thought about the question for a second then shook my head. "It's best if I don't," I said, chuckling as I took a sip of my ale, which turned out to taste exactly as I was afraid it would.

I nearly dropped the pewter cup when I'd swallowed a mouthful.

"This is beer!" I blurted out.

"Of course it is. What did you think it was?"

"I'm not allowed to drink alcohol!" I retorted. "I'm too young."

Lachlan laughed. "We're not in Fairhaven, Vega," he said. "You're allowed to do whatever you want here. You're a Seeker. A Summoner. A Shadow. A triple threat. Surely you can live it up a little for a few minutes. Besides, this isn't alcohol—not exactly. It's derived from a root found here in the Otherwhere. It will relax you a little, but it's not going to get you drunk or anything."

"It had better not." Much as the idea of feeling tipsy appealed to me, I wasn't sure I wanted to lose control over my senses in a place like this. This town felt far too dangerous.

"Drink it slowly. I promise, it won't do you any harm. At the very most, it'll loosen you up a little."

I narrowed my eyes at him before deciding I trusted him enough to take another sip, and another, until I finally began to genuinely enjoy the feeling of calm that was overtaking me.

We sat together for a time, talking and laughing about nothing in particular. I told myself not to think about what Lachlan had said—and *hadn't* said—about my scent. I tried not to make eye contact with him too frequently…and when I found myself struck by how handsome he was, I told myself it was the ale messing with my mind, and the fact that I was feeling vulnerable and missing Callum—which was definitely true.

I was about to ask Lachlan a question when someone came charging over from the opposite end of the room, startling me into immediate focus.

SINDOR

"Lachlan!" the man shouted, swatting my companion on the back before throwing me a curious look. "How the living hell are ya?"

"Good," he replied, gesturing toward me. "Sindor, this is...um, Shirley."

I shot him an amused look. *Quite the pseudonym.* I was pretty certain the last time anyone had actually been named Shirley was 1945.

"Very pleased to meet ya...Shirley," the man called Sindor replied, giving my hand a hearty shake.

He was short, with a very round, bald head. His cheeks were a splotchy red, as was his nose, and apart from a hint of flickering reflection in his eyes, he looked entirely human.

Lachlan leaned in close to our host and said, "We're here on very important business. But I'd appreciate if you'd keep that quiet. It's the sort of business that could attract the wrong kind of people, if you know what I mean."

"Of course, of course. You're looking for a room upstairs, I assume?"

"*Two* rooms," I corrected, probably a little more aggressively than I needed to.

"Hmm. Sorry, lass. The best I can do for ya both is a double. The place is all booked up for the Festival, of course."

"Festival?" Lachlan and I asked in unison.

"It's Haunted Eve," Sindor said, giving Lachlan a playful knock in the shoulder. "You really telling me you've forgotten?"

"Haunted Eve!" Lachlan repeated, smacking himself on the forehead. "I can't believe it. I did forget. It's been a long time."

"What's Haunted Eve?" I asked. I was tempted to ask if it bore any resemblance to Halloween in our world, but doing so would have given away too much about my origins.

"A massive drunken party," Sindor replied. "It takes place each year in these parts. A sort of celebration of Volkston's lack of humanity, if you will." He bit his lip after he'd said it. "No offense, lass. It's perfectly all right to be human, of course."

"None taken."

"There'll be a sort of makeshift party in the town's streets. Costumes, food, drink, the whole lot. You two ought really to go and watch. But..." He eyed me thoughtfully for a moment, "You should probably keep yourself covered, Shirley. Particularly your eyes. And it wouldn't hurt you to wear something that smells of your friend here, to cover up a bit of that, erm, lovely scent of yours."

I glanced at Lachlan, who nodded his agreement. "Sorry, but he's right. The men will be drunk—at least, some of them will. Probably wise not to throw the temptation of human flesh their way."

"Fine, then. Can I borrow your shirt?"

Lachlan let out a laugh and took a swig of his ale. "As long as I can borrow yours."

"Har har," I scoffed, unsure whether he was flirting with me as heavily as he seemed to be.

"Alternatively, I could just lock myself into the room," I suggested in a slightly cranky tone.

"Nonsense," Sindor shot back. "Lachlan here will take care of you. Won't you, lad?"

"Of course I will."

"Well, then, I'll leave you to it," Sindor told us with a wink. "Your room key will be waiting behind the front desk when the time comes. I'll let them know you're on your way."

"Thanks," I said with a smile.

Sindor shot me a final look before taking off for the other end of the pub.

"What would you like to do?" Lachlan asked, his tone sincere. "If you want to stay in the room, it's okay with me."

I thought about the question for a second, then shook my head. "No, of course not. We're here for a reason. We're looking for something, even if we don't know what it is. I suppose we may as well get out among the crowd and see what we can find out. Even if it means taking a bit of a risk."

"You're sure?"

"Pretty sure."

I took a large swig of my drink, then added, "Okay. Now I'm *really* sure."

CLOSE QUARTERS

When we'd acquired a room key from the young Grell working at the front desk, we headed upstairs to assess our sleeping quarters, which turned out to be cozy, to put it generously.

The room was at the far end of the third story's hallway. Its only bed was a narrow double, and the floor space on either side was barely wide enough to walk through. One small, soot-stained window overlooked the street below, which was currently crawling with pedestrians of all shapes and sizes.

The one positive was a long, narrow bathroom with a small door, tucked away like a closet in the far corner, which contained an ancient-looking clawfoot tub.

"I'd offer to sleep on the floor," Lachlan said, "but there's no room. If you like, I can crash in the stables, in wolf form. Straw's actually a very comfortable bed."

"No way," I said. "Don't be ridiculous. We're friends. We slept close together last night—we can do it again tonight. Besides, I'd be tossing and turning with guilt all night if you did that."

"I think you're forgetting that it was my wolf who slept next to you. He wouldn't exactly fit in this bed."

"So we'll just have to pretend you're a wolf tonight, too. It's fine."

But I wasn't sure I meant it. I'd never slept in a bed with anyone but Callum, and I wondered with horror if there was any chance I'd do something terrible in my sleep like roll over and accidentally kiss Lachlan.

Don't be stupid, I told myself. *Now you're just inventing cheesy scenes from Rom-coms. Surely you can sleep with another person without unintentionally playing tonsil hockey with them.*

We tossed our bags onto the room's sole chair before agreeing to take turns cleaning up in the diminutive bathroom. I was more than a little grateful for the opportunity to take a hot shower and change out of my sweaty riding clothes.

Before I headed in, Lachlan pulled off the shirt he'd been wearing and tossed it to me.

I tried my best not to gawk at his sculpted abdomen or powerful arms.

"Sorry," he said, "I know the shirt's not clean. But Sindor was right—you'd be better to smell a little of my kind than entirely human. If the wrong Waerg or Grell catches your scent...or if a Sasser were to show up..."

Sasser.

The hairs on the back of my neck stood on end with the mention of the word. Sassers were the deadly assassin-for-hire Waergs employed by Marauth, the wizard in Merriwether's order who was looking to stir up the Otherwhere's pecking order.

And their sole goal in life, it seemed, was to end mine.

I hadn't seen any of their ferocious kind since the day we'd hunted for the Lyre of Adair on the rocky shores of Cornwall.

And I would have been all too happy never to see one of their kind again.

When I'd showered and dried myself off, I pulled the shirt I'd borrowed from Lachlan over my head. As I waited for him to shower, I layered my cloak overtop, yanking the hood up in an attempt to hide myself in shadow.

"Hmm," Lachlan said when he'd returned to the bedroom to have a look at me. "I'm afraid you still stand out like a sore thumb. Even with the cloak and hood."

"What are you talking about? I'm hidden. Sort of."

"Well, first, there are your eyes, which are definitely not hidden."

"What about them?"

"They're distinctly human."

"You say that like it's a bad thing."

"Not at all bad. Just…striking." Lachlan gestured toward the window. "Look, the crowds out there are all wearing masks. Maybe you should, too."

"I don't have one. And I'm not sure what I can do to cover my eyes. Short of putting a pillowcase over my head, I mean."

"Here," Lachlan said, reaching for a white curtain that half-covered the window and pulling off the ribbon-like length of diaphanous fabric that tied it back. "Pull your hood down for a second."

When I did so, he positioned himself behind me to tie the fabric gently around my head. "Can you see through this?" he asked, his breath caressing my neck.

"I can," I said, my voice slightly strained. I twisted around to face him. "But don't I look a little weird like this?"

Through the mostly-transparent material, I could see the corners of Lachlan's lips pulling themselves up into a smile. "You look beautiful, actually."

When I tightened, he added, "Not to mention that you'll fit right in. Just look out the window. You'll see what I mean."

I peeked out only to see that the crowd milling about below was beginning to alter from strolling pedestrians to a parade of costumed creatures, one more bizarre than the next. They wore everything from distorted, human-looking faces to full-on papier mâché animal heads four or five times the size of their own.

"So this celebration is something like a Carnival," I said. "It looks like New Orleans during Mardi Gras or something."

"Or something," Lachlan agreed, gazing over my shoulder at the street below. I could feel how close he was, though I couldn't exactly blame him for it. There wasn't any room to spare in our tiny rented space.

"What are *you* going to wear?" I asked, twisting away from him to seat myself on the bed.

"I don't have a lot of options, so I think I'll just wear my wolf's face," he said. "It'll be easier to move through the crowd together if it's obvious that one of us is at home here. They'll more likely notice me than you, and they'll assume you're one of my pack...hopefully."

"Fair enough. Let's go, then," I said. "The sooner we get out there and figure out if there's anyone in this town who can help us, the sooner we can come back and get a good night's rest."

MAREYA

WHEN WE'D LOCKED up the room, we headed down to the street, where Lachlan shifted into his wolf form to pad along next to me.

"I have no idea where to go," I murmured as we turned right and squeezed our way between two tall Grells in face masks who were coming toward us. "And *you* can't talk. So I'm just going to put my hand on your back, and you steer us, okay?"

Lachlan let out a low sort of growl and pressed himself close to me. I buried my fingers in his coat and let him guide me along the street, where shops, pubs, and bistros were lit up brightly, their doors and windows wide open, inviting passersby to come in and enjoy their wares.

The scent of baked goods wafted through the air, reminding me how little we'd eaten since leaving the Academy. But rather than succumb to a craving for treats slathered in butter, we kept moving.

When my eyes landed on a strange-looking shop called "Mareya's Curiosities," I could no longer resist the urge to take a look.

"Let's stop," I said. "Can we go inside? Something about this place is calling my name."

A second later, Lachlan was standing next to me again in his human form. "Literally?" he asked, "or figuratively?"

"The second one."

"In that case, let's go," he said, gesturing to me to enter.

I slipped inside, the white gauze still covering my eyes, and began to peruse the cluttered but charming tables and shelves set up inside the shop.

Most of the items on hand were small trinkets. A mortar and pestle here, an intricate silver-and-stone pendant there. Books of spells and incantations lined the walls, and occasionally my eyes would land on a painted skull or a set of bones on display, none of which looked entirely human.

"This place reminds me a little of my Nana's house," I said as we strolled through the shop. "You've seen her cottage, of course. She always has the wildest assortment of magical-looking items lying around."

"Is there anything here that draws your eye?" Lachlan asked quietly. "Anything that pulls you in?"

I was about to say *no* when the thick red leather spine of a book drew my eye to a shelf just above my head. I reached up and pulled it down to examine it.

"Dragons of the North," I mouthed, reading the title.

"Seems like a good start," Lachlan replied with a smile.

Pulling the book open, my eyes landed on a hand-drawn map, presumably of the Otherwhere. I'd never actually seen it laid out in front of me before, and I found myself fascinated by the shape of the realm.

"It's an island!" I said, turning to Lachlan. "I don't know why I never realized that." I traced my finger over a few spots. "Here's the Academy in the east—the mountains to the west...and look, there's Kaer Uther in the southeast. So *that's* where Uldrach is..."

"You've been to all those places, I take it?" he asked. "You've seen them?"

"I have. But I got to them through Breaches—I mean, the doors I'd summoned. Never by walking or riding. I guess I never realized how big the Otherwhere was. Or how *small*. It looks a little like England, when I think about it. But entirely different, too. England doesn't have mountains like the Five Sisters, for one thing."

I stared for a few seconds at the north-western corner of the land. To the north of the mountains, which formed a sort of impossible, massive circle in the Otherwhere's western region, the map showed little in the way of detail other than a hint of snow and ice.

It was almost like someone had forgotten to finish mapping it out and the north-western corner had been lost in the process.

One word was written over the region, above what looked like a drawing of a large stone cliff face at the base of a tall mountain.

"What's this area?" I asked, pointing to it. "It looks like it says *Dragonhelm*?"

"They used to say the dragons made their home in the land beyond the mountains," a low, smooth female voice said from behind me. "It was a place to escape to when they'd freed themselves of their human bonds."

Shocked, I spun around to see that a woman was staring at me.

Her eyes were yellow like amber, her hair jet-black and as shiny as satin. Her cheekbones were high and pronounced, like those of a wild cat.

A Grell?

She had to be. No human could look that feline.

Though unlike most Grells I'd seen, she wasn't furry.

"My name is Mareya," she said, raising her chin. "I own this shop."

"Ah," I replied, thinking quickly. "I'm Ve...Veronica. And this is...Archie."

Lachlan threw me a puzzled but amused look.

The woman's lips twisted into a sly smile. "Pleased to meet you, Archie and Veronica," she said. "Tell me, what do you wish to know of the dragons who dwell in the north?"

I hesitated for a moment, then decided it probably wouldn't hurt to give her a little information. "I want to know where a dragon might go if he was trying to hide. Particularly a very *powerful* dragon."

"Ah. Well, you don't need me for that," Mareya said, pointing to Dragonhelm on the map. "They say there is a cavern in that part of the Otherwhere—one that is occupied by only the strongest of their kind at any given time."

"The strongest? How do dragons determine that?"

She looked straight into my eyes and said, "Combat, of course. The winner, as they say, takes all." A moment later, she laughed and added, "Unless, of course, a challenger comes along who is so powerful that no other dragon dare take him on. In fact, I hear a new beast has been spotted over the mountains. They say he is magnificent—the color of a golden crown."

My heart leaping in my chest, I pulled my eyes to Lachlan, who reached out and put a hand on my arm as if to calm me down before I said something incredibly stupid.

Settle down, Veronica.

"When...did this golden dragon first appear?" I asked.

"Tell me, why are you so interested?" Mareya asked, sniffing the air as if trying to figure out exactly who and what I was. "What does a girl such as yourself have to do with a dragon?"

"Everything," I blurted out without thinking.

I could feel Lachlan tensing next to me, but Mareya smiled again.

"I believe I understand," she said, tilting her head as if reading me. "As I'm sure you know, a dragon only becomes an independent creature when he is severed from a human. The golden beast must have left his human counterpart recently. You know the young man. You want him to become whole again, and you are seeking the way."

Before I could respond, Lachlan stepped forward. "With respect, we'd prefer to keep our business to ourselves," he said. "Tell me, how much do you want for the book Ve—Veronica—has got in her hands?"

Mareya eyed the red volume. "Fifty gold pieces."

"That's insane," Lachlan snarled. "Highway robbery."

Mareya sneered. "The gold is for my silence. You can have the *book* for nothing."

"I only want the map," I told her, pulling out the sack of coins from inside my cloak and beginning to count them out. "I don't care about the money. You can have it."

"Fine, then. Tear the map out. And if I may offer you a piece of advice…"

"Yes?" I asked, despite the fact that I could feel Lachlan growing more agitated by the second.

"Make your way toward the realm of the Witches, my dear. They will help you. They are, I fear, the only ones who can—regardless of what anyone may tell you."

"Seek them out?" I asked, trying in vain to read her expression. "Isn't that a bad idea? I thought the Witches were…not the nicest people in the world."

"Ah," Mareya chuckled. "You're the sort that thinks my kind turns people into toads and puts curses on them."

My kind?

My mouth dropped open. "I'm sorry—I didn't realize. I just assumed you were a Grell."

"A Grell!" she laughed. "I suppose it's the feline features, is it?"

"No, it was…I mean…I don't know."

"Don't you?"

Mareya laughed again, and then, with the briefest flash of light, she vanished.

Lachlan elbowed me gently and nodded toward the floor.

Confused, I looked down to see a sleek black cat with golden eyes staring up at us.

"She's a shifter?" I asked.

A second later, Mareya was standing in front of us again. "Waergs aren't the only ones who morph into other forms. Then again, you already know that. I believe you have met a warlock, have you not...Vega Sloane?"

A powerful shiver overtook me to hear my name on her lips.

In that moment, nothing mattered. Not the veil I was wearing over my eyes, or the camouflage-cloak, or Lachlan's scent-masking shirt. I felt like this woman—this Mareya—could see right through me.

I may as well have been nothing but a pile of bones and organs for her to dig through.

"I have met a warlock, yes," I said. "But I don't want to talk about him."

"Of course you don't." Mareya turned away and picked up a small crystal ball from the counter next to her. Gazing into its depths, she added, "Lumus is not a kind man. He thrives on cruelty, in fact. You will see him again, of course. But by the time you do, you will have changed."

"Changed?"

"In ways you cannot yet imagine."

I felt Lachlan's hand on my back as if for support, and I was grateful. Something in the way the Witch was predicting an uncertain future made me feel instantly weakened.

"I need to find the dragon," I said, trying to ignore her ominous tone. "It's important—not just for me, but for the Otherwhere. That's all that matters."

"Journey to the land of my Sisters, then," she said abruptly, her gaze intense as she stared at me. "At the base of Sorella—the second highest peak in the region. If you come upon them, tell them what it is that you seek. They may help you. They may not. But you will not pass the mountains to Dragonhelm without their consent and their blessing. They will not allow it."

"Thank you," I said. "We will look for them."

"I did not say to *look* for them."

"Okay, now I'm just confused…how am I supposed to find them, then?"

"They will find you. No one can find the Coven, unless the Witches wish to be found." Without explaining herself further, Mareya turned to Lachlan. "You," she said in a mysterious tone, "are difficult to read. You are more than a mere Waerg. More than you think you are. But there is one who sees your potential. One who will elevate you as you deserve."

"I don't know what you're talking about," he snapped, wincing as if she was hurting him with her words.

"You *will* know, young man," she said with a teasing wink.

"We should leave," he said, taking me by the arm. I could feel him silently imploring me, as if something in the Witch's tone had set off an explosion inside him.

I handed over fifty gold coins and thanked Mareya before tearing the map from the book, which I left behind.

"Be careful on this night, both of you," she said as we headed for the door. "There are some in this town who would not wish for the two of you to see the sun rise again."

FIREWORKS

"You said too much about our business back there," Lachlan reprimanded when we'd stepped out onto the street and had begun to walk. "*Way* too much."

Music was blaring all around us from some unseen source. Whether it was the partygoers singing and playing concealed instruments, or electronic speakers somewhere along the shops' façades, I couldn't tell. The melody was frantically energetic and inspired the creatures around us to dance and skip in wild, frenetic movements.

But I was barely aware of them as Lachlan's eyes, cold and unblinking, glared into the distance.

"I said what I needed to," I told him. "I had to get some information from her."

"From a Witch?" Lachlan scoffed. "You actually think one of their kind is going to tell you the truth?"

I stopped walking and grabbed his arm, turning him toward me. He was breathing heavily, his nostrils flaring with what looked like serious agitation.

"I do think she was truthful, yes," I told him.

"Oh, come on, Vega. Are you really that naive?"

"Maybe I am," I replied. "What did she mean in there, when she said you're more than a mere Waerg, anyway? Is that what's got you all riled up?"

Lachlan clenched his jaw, turned, and began walking again. "It doesn't matter what she said," he snarled as I caught up. "But I'm sure it doesn't mean anything. People like her are con artists. Scammers. She wants our money for looking into crystal balls and reading our palms. She managed to get fifty gold coins out of you for a *map*, for God's sake."

"I think you're wrong," I said. "I think she knows a lot, and you don't want to admit it because of what it might mean for you."

"Oh? And what exactly might it mean, Little Miss Clairvoyant?"

"I don't know," I confessed. "But what if she's right? What if you're something more than just a Waerg?"

"Just a Waerg," he huffed. "Wow. I didn't realize you thought so little of me."

"I didn't mean it like that," I said.

"Of course you didn't. I'm sure you think I'm the greatest guy in the world, right? For a *Waerg*."

"Lachlan..." Once again, I grabbed him, halting him in his tracks. But this time he wouldn't look at me. "Look, I'm sorry. I said something stupid. You know I think the world of you. I only meant—"

"You only meant I'm a member of an inferior species," he spat.

"What's your problem, really?" I asked. "You're angry about something, but I think it's more than just me blurting out thoughtless words."

"They...*Witches*...hate my kind. They judge us. They think we're nothing more than animals, in the worst sense of the word."

"If they hated your kind, why would someone like Mareya be living in a town full of Waergs?"

"People often live among those they hate," he said, his tone acrid. "You know that as well as I do. It doesn't mean much."

"Lachlan," I said, trying to calm my agitated voice. "I get it. You're angry with her. With me. If this is too much for you—all of this—if you want to go home, you can. But I'm going to the mountains. I'm finishing this."

"I'm not—" he stammered, shaking his head.

"You're not what?"

"I'm not leaving you," he said, reaching for my hand.

I let him take it, and we stood there, silently staring at one another like the world wasn't in a raucous state of mayhem and noise around us, costumed Waergs and Grells dancing by in blissful ignorance of our seemingly trivial conflict.

After a few seconds, Lachlan let go. "I mean, it wouldn't be right to let you travel alone. I promised to look out for you, and I will. Witches or not."

"I know you promised. But I'm not going to hold you to it. If you don't want to come, it's fine."

"Well, you *should* hold me to it. A promise is a promise." With that, he turned and began walking again. "I'm hungry. Let's find somewhere to eat."

"Wait—*why* should I hold you to it?" I asked, unwilling to drop the subject. "Why should I expect anything of you, considering all you've done for me?"

"Because I'm not a guy who breaks my vows. I'm not a guy who just betrays people. And because..." He pursed his lips tight then let out a rough breath. "Because I need you to know I'd do anything for you."

Instead of asking anything more, I turned my focus to the storefronts around us, pushing away the unwelcome feeling of intimacy that was bubbling up inside me.

"That place looks good," I said after we'd walked another half a block, gesturing to a restaurant with a large black bird on its sign. "The Onyx Crow."

"As long as they don't *serve* crow, I'm in," Lachlan agreed, and we headed for the door.

The scent of savory meat pie greeted our noses as we stepped inside, and we tacitly agreed that we'd made an excellent choice.

We headed for a table in the corner, away from the other clients. Most of them were male—some Grells, others Waergs, all of them at least half drunk. The conversation was loud, their intoxicated voices bellowing through the low-ceilinged space in an aggressive yet friendly cacophony.

A few eyes turned my way as we passed by, and I wondered if they, like Mareya, knew exactly who and what I was.

"I feel like I need to sniff my armpits," I muttered as I squeezed in close to Lachlan in an attempt to conceal myself.

"Don't worry," he said as we sat down, "you smell fine. Like a slightly-better-than-average Waerg, I'd say. They're probably just surprised to see a woman in here."

"A woman," I repeated. I was so accustomed to being called a girl that I wasn't sure what to make of the title.

When we'd ordered some steak, sausage, and potatoes, I pulled out the map I'd torn out of the book at Mareya's shop and laid it flat on the table. "Is it okay to look at this in such a public place?" I asked.

"Sure," Lachlan said. "As long as we don't drop the D-word too much."

"Dingus?"

"Dragon."

"I know, silly."

He smiled for the first time in what felt like ages.

"Look, Vega…" he began, but I shushed him.

"I don't want things to be awkward between us," I said. "Can we just acknowledge that right now, you're just about the most important person in my life, and I really appreciate that you're here, whatever that means?"

He nodded, gestured as if zipping up his lips, and leaned in to look at the map.

"Okay," I said. "According to this, I was right to think we're a couple of days' ride from the mountains. It'll probably take a day or two more after that to get anywhere close to the area called Dragonhelm. That is, if the Witches let us pass." I shot Lachlan a look to see if he'd react with horror, but he stayed calm. "After that, who knows what will happen?"

"Who knows?" he repeated in a less than enthusiastic tone.

I folded up the map and changed the subject to the likely weather over the next few days, which seemed to cheer him up somewhat.

After we'd finished our meal, we headed back out to the street. By now, it was crawling with fully costumed locals wearing everything from elaborate headpieces to nothing at all, in the case of a couple of Grells who were furry enough that clothing didn't seem particularly necessary.

A loud, sudden bang startled me, and I found myself reaching for the hilt of my blade before Lachlan grabbed my arm and shook his head. "It's all right," he said, nodding up the road. "They're just setting off some fireworks. Come on, let's go have a look."

When a sea of lights exploded in the sky above the distant rooftops, I let out a laugh. "Wow. Okay, I guess I need to relax a little."

"Yes. You really do. Maybe I should have bought you some more ale. Or a more powerful sedative."

With another chuckle, I accompanied him up the road, which ascended toward what looked like a squat fortress at its highest point. Above the structure, fireworks continued to explode in beautiful displays of swirling light, forming exquisitely crafted silhouettes of animals: a deer's head with majestic antlers. A bear. A family of rabbits. A wolf.

And finally, a massive dragon.

Seeing the creature sent my heart racing. I knew the image was fleeting—only a temporary illusion—but its outline was so familiar, with its far-spread wings, snaking tail, and long, arching neck.

For a moment, I was certain I saw its wings flap slowly. It was alive, soaring through the sky as I'd seen Callum do so many times in his dragon form in the days before I'd known Caffall's name.

When the dragon had faded to nothing, I sighed, hugging my arms around my shoulders.

"It's cold," I said absently.

Lachlan positioned himself half-behind me, pressing himself to me to keep me warm. After he realized I wasn't going to recoil from him, he wrapped an arm around me from behind. Exhausted, I let my head rest against him for a few seconds before finally pulling away.

"Sorry," he said. "I just wanted to warm you up."

"I know. It's fine. It's just..." I turned to face him, looking up into his reflective green eyes. "You know."

"I do," he mouthed with a shallow smile. "But as I've said, I'm not trying to steal you, Vega. Much as I'd like to."

"No. You're too good to try that," I said. "A Waerg with a conscience. A caring, non-predatorial wolf who chooses to coddle the lamb, rather than slaughter it."

"That's me."

I stood next to him until the display was over, my eyes occasionally veering to one of the passing townsfolk. Every now and then, I'd catch one of them slowing down as he or she passed me, sniffing the air as if detecting something that wasn't quite right.

But they always continued along their way, once they'd shot Lachlan a look and confirmed that all was as it should be.

When the fireworks had finally concluded with an explosive grand finale which involved a full-on battle in the sky between

Grells, Waergs, and humans, we turned to begin the walk back to the inn.

"We should get some sleep," Lachlan told me. "Long day ahead tomorrow if we're going to make a real push toward the mountains."

"Mmm," I said with a yawn, which I stifled with the back of my hand. "Definitely. Sleep would be—"

My words were violently cut off when Lachlan grabbed me and shoved me hard against the façade of the shop next to us. He pressed a hand against the wall to the right of my face and fixed his eyes on mine, his chest heaving.

"Don't move," he whispered, "and please…forgive me for this."

Without another word, he cupped my chin in his hand and pressed his lips to mine.

SASSER

FOR THE BRIEFEST moment I found myself too confused to resist.

Once my head had cleared, I pressed my hands to Lachlan's chest and tried—and failed—to shove him away.

He pulled back only an inch or two, his breath misting the air between us.

"Why the hell did you do that?" I asked, rolling my hands into fists.

"No time to explain. Look into my eyes and pretend I'm making you laugh."

"What? Why?"

"Do it. Trust me, Vega. Just one more time."

Reluctantly, I let out a ringing giggle, as if he'd just told the most hysterical joke I'd ever heard, and he pressed his face to my neck like he was about to kiss me again.

His lips fluttered along my skin as he muttered, "There's a Sasser coming up the street from your left. I don't know if he's hunting you and me—but he's definitely after *someone*. Laugh again, but keep your face near mine."

I did as he asked, though this time, the sound was far more forced.

"What do we do?" I asked, pulling my chin down, my cheek pressed to his.

"Don't move," he said, pulling himself closer. "I'm trying my best to cover up your scent with my own. It's why I kissed you. Your breath—it smells...very human."

"I have no idea if that's an insult or not," I replied.

"It's not an insult," he said.

"Good. I think. God, I'm so confused right now." I put my arms around his waist and pulled him tight to my body, peeking out over his shoulder through my gauzy blindfold. "Not to mention that I want to punch you so hard that it's killing me."

I could see a man now, skulking up the street toward us as the Grells and Waergs in his path moved out of the way to let him pass, like they, too, could sense his nefarious intentions.

The man had bright yellow eyes and brown hair that hung over his forehead in a greasy fringe. His jaw was square, and I might have called him handsome if not for the fact that his face seemed set in a permanent scowl.

I pressed myself to Lachlan, petrified, my arms fully around him now. I wasn't supposed to use my magical skills. No disappearing. No summoning. All I had for protection was a dagger called Murphy and a Waerg who was loyal to a fault.

Both of Lachlan's hands were holding me by the waist now, and he was leaning into me, pressing his cheek to mine like a cat rubbing its scent on a person it had decided to claim. My hands were tangled in his hair, trying to absorb his scent onto every exposed inch of my skin.

"We shouldn't have come out," I breathed into his ear. "I was stupid to think it was a good idea."

"Don't speak," he whispered, and once again I could feel his lips on my skin, leaving a trail of reluctant goosebumps in their wake. "Don't show fear. Just...try to relax. I know it's hard."

I nodded, trying to embrace the feel of his skin against mine.

I'm not enjoying this, I told myself. *But everything I'm doing—*

every breath, every step, every second I'm touching Lachlan—it's all for Callum. I'm here to find a way to get him back. That's all.

With those semi-reassuring words floating through my mind, I finally began to relax, pressing my face to Lachlan's. His breath caressed my earlobe, his chest heaving.

To anyone passing, it must have looked as though we were making out passionately. And I didn't much care, as long as it kept us alive long enough to accomplish our goal.

Holding my breath, I watched as the Sasser trudged by us. Lachlan's body was still pressed tight to mine, and I hardly dared blink for fear that it would send my scent wafting in the killer's direction.

When I watched him disappear around a corner some distance away, I finally allowed myself to exhale.

"He's gone?" Lachlan asked.

I nodded.

He pulled back, letting out a slow breath, his eyes meeting my own.

"I'm really sorry," he said. "Again."

"You were my cloaking device, and it seems that you worked. I can forget the kiss if you can."

"I…" he replied, "I can try, but I can't exactly promise anything. Come on—I think we're going to have to cut our night short."

He took my hand and led me back to the inn at a half-jog that didn't let up until we'd stepped into our room and locked the door behind us.

"I need to find a way to keep you safe," he said, chewing on his thumbnail as he paced the narrow gap between the bed and the window. "I can't let those bastards get so close to you again, Vega. I need to find another way."

"It's okay," I told him. "We're safe now."

He stopped his pacing and looked at me. His eyes brightened in the dark like a fire had flared to life inside him.

"I think they know," he said.

"Know what?"

"I think Marauth—maybe the Usurper Queen, too—knows about the golden dragon. About Caffall. If Mareya knew, that means word has gotten out. Everyone will be hunting him. Which means they'll be hunting you, too."

"Me? Why hunt me? Aside from Mareya, no one even knows I'm here."

"Because you're the only one who stands a chance of bringing Callum and his dragon back together. If you succeed…"

"Callum survives," I said.

"And if you fail…"

"He dies."

He nodded. "There's no way to be sure that Sasser was after you. But we need to leave first thing tomorrow and ride as long as we can. It might well be another three days until we reach the mountains. We'll need to be vigilant."

Freaked out, I nodded. There was nothing to say. He was right; I was probably going to be stalked through the Otherwhere, and the best we could hope for was to evade our pursuers long enough to find some real answers.

"My entire life since I turned seventeen has been one day after another of psychotic creatures trying to murder me," I said. "But this is the first time it's been over something other than a magical hidden object."

With that, I let out a chuckle.

"What's funny?" Lachlan asked, his brow furrowed like he was mildly annoyed.

"It's just…I haven't thought about the Relics since we left the Academy. I mean, Merriwether has the Sword of Viviane and the Lyre now. But there are two more Relics out there, and I can't even bring myself to think about them. Is that weird?"

"Not weird," Lachlan replied. "You have other things on your mind. Besides, don't the Relics sort of reveal themselves to you in their own time?"

"Kind of. In bits and pieces. They always seem to steer my life in strange ways. I find it's best not to give them too much thought, or I could drive myself mad."

"I only meant that the world and fate work in strange and mysterious ways."

"Don't you dare say *fate*," I growled, half joking. "It's the F-word I hate most in this world. It's supposedly fate that took Callum away. It's fate that left my grandparents separated from one another for life. Fate is an unholy, smelly bitch-goddess, and I'd smack her in her smug little face if I could."

"Okay, but how do you *really* feel?"

We stared at each other for a moment, then both burst out laughing.

"This is so ridiculous," I said, wiping a tear away as I tried to regain control over myself. "I first learned about the Otherwhere in late July. That was, what, four months ago, and how many things have gone horribly wrong in my life? I must be setting some kind of record here."

"Trust me—I'm sure many, many more things will go horribly wrong yet."

"Damn you for that," I chuckled.

"Seriously, Vega—you've been through hell and lived to tell the tale. That's got to be worth something, right?"

"Sure," I sighed. "Listen, I'm going to take a bath before bed. Okay if I take over the bathroom for a few minutes?"

"Of course. I'll be here waiting and watching. I mean, not watching you bathe. I'll be...watching the street." Tongue-tied and clearly embarrassed, Lachlan rolled his eyes at himself. "You know what I mean."

"I know, you weirdo."

I threw him a quick smile, grateful for his watchful eye, and headed into the bathroom, where the narrow clawfoot tub awaited me.

When I'd filled it with steaming hot water, I climbed in and washed away the thick layer of anxiety, fear, and guilt that was eating away at me.

I'd kissed Lachlan tonight.

Except that I hadn't.

He'd kissed *me*.

And in doing so, he might have saved my life.

I closed my eyes, leaned back, and tried not to think about it.

The only problem was, I still had one difficulty to navigate before morning:

Our sleeping arrangements.

FLAME

When I'd finished bathing and changed into a pair of shorts and a t-shirt, I slipped into the bed to tuck myself under a thin quilt.

The room was dark, and Lachlan still stood silhouetted by the window, watching the noisy passersby enjoying themselves outside.

I could hear music, shouting, and the general atmosphere of celebration on the street below, though it wasn't nearly as loud or raucous as I'd feared it would be. The festival run by those who were half animal, it seemed, was more civilized than most of the drunken human gatherings I'd ever witnessed.

"I think I may actually get some sleep tonight," I said, stretching my arms over my head.

"Good. I hope you do," Lachlan replied, but he didn't take his eyes off the street outside.

"What do you see out there that's got you so fascinated?" I asked, pressing my head into the pillow and closing my eyes.

"Nothing out of the ordinary. Just Grells and Waergs, enjoying themselves on a pleasant night."

"So why are you staring?"

"Because I *feel* something," he said quietly, a hint of alarm tingeing his voice.

My eyes popped open, and I turned to look at him, nervous. "You feel something? Do I even want to know what you mean by that?" This wasn't going to be some emotional declaration that would make the night ahead even more awkward...was it?

"I feel...nervous." He turned my way finally, setting his eyes on me. "Too many people know our business in this town. Too many eyes have been on us. Too many noses, picking up our scents."

"Oh," I said, closing my eyes again. "That. It's fine. We're fine. We managed to hide from that Sasser. I'm not worried."

"I can't believe I'm saying this to you of all people—but you're too confident."

"Exhaustion makes me confident, I guess. Now get some rest. I don't want to be picking your drooling body up off the ground when you fall off Dudley in the middle of our ride tomorrow."

With a growl of protest, Lachlan headed into the bathroom to brush his teeth. A few minutes later, I could hear him rifling through one of the bags sitting on the chair near the foot of the bed.

"What are you doing?" I asked, pushing myself up onto my elbows.

"Making sure we're set to leave first thing in the morning," he replied. "I don't want us leaving anything important behind."

"You do worry too much. Come on. The bed is actually quite comfortable. You really should relax."

"That's more easily said than done, Vega."

But a few seconds later, he climbed into bed next to me. I could feel his body heat, but was grateful that he managed to squeeze his large frame under the quilt without actually making physical contact.

"Good night," I said with another yawn, grateful for his gentlemanly behavior.

"Night, Vega," he replied, rolling onto his side away from me. "I'll wake you at dawn."

"Mmm," I replied, just barely registering the words.

As I slept, dreams invaded my mind, of frigid mountain trails and howling wolves.

At one point, I was walking through a blizzard, blinded by a sea of horizontally blowing snow. I called out for Lachlan, desperate to know where he was—I cried his name over and over—but he never came. I was alone, and all I could see was a ball of flame shooting through the sky in the distance like a falling star.

Or was it a dragon?

I shot up in bed, drenched in sweat and breathing hard, only to see what looked like the flickering glow of orange flames dancing just outside the window.

"Oh, my God!" I cried, grabbing Lachlan's shoulder and waking him. "Get up!"

A second later, we were both on our feet, and he was pressed to the window, staring out.

"The inn's on fire!" he yelled, grabbing my bag off the nearby chair and tossing it my way. "Quick! We need to get to the horses and get out of here!"

For some reason, instead of following his advice, I darted over and looked out the window.

The street below was dark, but the yellow-orange reflections on the windows across the way revealed a wall of flame dancing its way up the inn's façade toward the very window where I was standing.

I scanned the cobbled road, looking for any sign of life.

The only person I saw stood on the far side of the street, where a pair of yellow eyes stared up at me, malevolent and twinkling.

"Mareya?" I murmured as Lachlan grabbed my arm and began to drag me toward the door. "But why would she…"

"We don't have time to speculate," he said. "Come on!"

I shuddered myself into alertness, nodded, and followed him out of the room and down the hallway toward the stairs. The innkeeper, Sindor, meanwhile, was banging on doors, waking the guests and calling out for them to get out while they still could.

When we'd sprinted down to the main floor, it became abundantly clear that the fire had started at the front of the inn. The entire front wall was a conflagration, the door consumed by flame.

Coughing our way through the pub on the first story, we found our way to the back through a tornado of swirling embers, and raced out into a small courtyard where we could hear frightened horses snorting and neighing in terror. No doubt they knew how close they were to a horrific death.

So fast that I was overwhelmed by his skill, Lachlan managed to locate Dudley and Phair's bridles and saddles. We led the horses outside, and while I held them, Lachlan raced back into the stable and opened the doors to the other stalls to free the rest of the horses, who jogged gratefully into the courtyard.

An alleyway wound its way from the courtyard toward the edge of the small town, and we led the horses along, grateful when the air seemed to cool down and the scent of burning wood left our noses.

"You all right?" Lachlan asked, his breath misting in front of his face when we were able to take a second to catch our breath. The inn's liberated horses were trotting by us toward a small open field in the distance, no doubt looking for the same relief we'd sought.

"Fine," I replied, staring back toward the town's center, which was now sending up an ominous cloud of smoke that reflected orange against the dark sky. "But I'm starting to understand why *Witch* is such a bad word."

"You don't know that Mareya did this," Lachlan said, lifting Phair's saddle onto the black horse's back as I held onto his halter. "She had no reason to. She's the one who wanted us to go see her 'Sisters.'"

"What? You're defending her now, after all your talk last night?"

"I'm just saying there are more likely culprits. The Sasser we saw earlier, for one."

"I saw her in the street, staring right up at our room," I said. "She looked like she was...I don't know, amused or something."

"Still..." Lachlan looked like he wanted to argue, but instead, he handed me Phair's bridle. "We have a long way to go, and the sooner we disappear from this place, the better. Let them think we died and our horses ran off."

When we'd finished tacking up the horses, I leapt onto Phair's back and followed Lachlan as he steered Dudley toward the western edge of town via another series of alleyways and narrow streets.

I'd told myself many times over the last few months that I was insane to have willingly walked into this strange new life of mine. And now, we were heading toward the mountains, seeking a Coven of Witches.

Even though one of their own had just tried to burn us alive.

I was *definitely* insane.

ATTACK

We rode for what felt like ages, weaving across streams, down ravines, and along long-abandoned roads that were half overgrown with vegetation.

Over the course of the first two hours or so, I must have twisted around at least a hundred times to look behind us.

Lachlan, on the other hand, appeared calm and collected, though every now and then I noticed him surreptitiously lifting his chin to sniff the air.

"We're alone," he finally said around eleven a.m. when he caught me once again scouring the woods with my eyes. "We're all right. Let's dismount and give the horses a break."

I nodded, and we got off and led the horses to a nearby stream to drink. The water was crystal clear and refreshing-looking, the air crisp, and aside from the fact that I was convinced we were going to be murdered, it was an exquisite day.

My hands, though, were raw with angry-looking blisters and newly forming calluses. "I should have worn gloves," I lamented as I looked at my fingers, wincing. "I'd forgotten that riders usually do."

"Let me see," Lachlan said, stepping over and taking my hands carefully in his. When he'd looked at them for a minute, he headed over to Dudley and pulled something out of his saddle bag.

"What's that?" I asked as he approached with a small glass jar.

"Healing balm. Someone packed it for us—I suspect that was Niala's doing."

He asked me to hold my hands up once again, and, unscrewing the jar's lid, he applied a clear gel to the open wounds in my flesh.

Almost immediately, the sting went away, and the angry inflammation around the blisters faded. The open sores sealed themselves as if they'd never been there.

"She's amazing," I said with a smile. "I always forget she's a magician in her own right."

"She is," Lachlan agreed. "And she cares about you a lot."

"I care about her, too."

When he'd finished with the balm, I asked, "What about you? Are your hands okay?"

"They're fine," he replied, holding them up to prove it. He was right. Aside from a little redness, they were unscathed. He had the hands of someone who knew manual labor. Rough and experienced, covered in thick-looking calluses.

"That's impressive," I said.

"It's a symptom of my nature, I suppose," Lachlan said with a grin. "My wolf's paws are thick to the point of being almost impenetrable. I suppose it translates to my hands."

Satisfied that he really was okay, I pulled the map of the Otherwhere from Mareya's shop out of my pocket and unfolded it, crouching down to set it on a dry patch of ground.

"Where are we?" I asked, staring at it.

"Here," Lachlan said, pointing to a spot near an east-west running river. "I'd say we have two nights to spend in the woods before we get to the base of the nearest mountain."

"Two nights," I sighed. "I'm at the point where I just want to summon a door and bring us there now. It feels like so much wasted time."

"Not wasted. If we'd gone through a Breach, we would never have met Mareya. Never have gotten the advice she gave us to head to the Coven."

"Before she tried to kill us in our sleep, you mean?"

Lachlan frowned. "I really think you have it wrong, Vega."

I'd clammed up and resisted arguing back in Volkston, but I could no longer hold back. "Come on. She knew about us. She had a motive, too."

"Oh? What was it?"

I shrugged. "Maybe the Witches want to find the dragon themselves. Cast a spell on him or something. Who knows? For whatever reason, she wants to keep us away from Caffall."

"The only ones with clear motives are the Sassers, or the Usurper Queen's Waergs," Lachlan said. "It's far more likely that one of them tried to kill us."

"Either way, I'm not thrilled about the idea of riding two days, then walking up to a bunch of Witches and saying, "Hey, so it's possible that one of your own tried to barbecue us in our sleep, but do you think you could help us out?"

"Well, the alternative is to walk up to Caffall, who could much more easily burn us alive, and ask him to somehow meld himself with Callum, even though apparently that's impossible. At least the Witches might have some kind of solution."

"The difference is that Caffall might actually listen to us."

"Or he might not. Do you really want to find out what would happen if he decided he didn't want our company?"

I stared out at the woods, mulling the thought. I'd met Caffall, of course, but only when Callum was alive inside him. He was alone now—a solitary, wild, independent creature. And I had no way of knowing if he was hostile or friendly.

"I suppose you're right," I said.

"You'll figure out one of these days that I'm always right, Sloane," Lachlan replied with a chuckle. "Come on, let's have a snack, then hit the non-road."

"Fine."

After a quick bite, we remounted and headed west once again.

A few times, I spotted quiet, well-maintained paths and dirt roads cutting through the woods, but each time, Lachlan steered us away, shaking his head quietly.

"Too much potential to run into enemies," he told me. "We're best sticking to the forest."

Which meant nervous horses trying to make their way among brambles, low-hanging branches, deep holes in the ground and rocky, uneven terrain.

Around six p.m. we finally set up camp in a clearing by a narrow, rushing river. As with our last outdoor camp-out, we chose not to set a fire, but instead ate more of the dried food we had with us and drank water from the river.

Dudley and Phair were calm and quiet, and for once, I didn't feel on edge about any threats that might come at us.

We slept better than expected under the stars. Lachlan had shifted into his wolf form once again, curled up around me to keep me from freezing.

I'd long since given up on the idea of feeling guilty for being close to him. Something told me Callum would not only understand, but would likely shake Lachlan's hand and thank him for his service.

Anything to give us some hope of ever finding one another again.

THE FOLLOWING day was blissfully quiet and uneventful. We made good progress on relatively easy terrain and camped out once again, this time with an encouraging view of the distant peaks to the west.

"Tomorrow, we go to see the Witches," Lachlan told me when we'd dismounted for the evening. "Assuming we can actually find them."

"What time tomorrow?" I asked, nervously excited.

"Probably late morning, if we get an early start."

We didn't talk much that evening. I told myself it was exhaustion that kept us from communicating, but if I was to be honest with myself, I had to admit that it came down to fear. I didn't want to argue about the Witches—about whether we thought they might be friends or enemies.

Mareya was a strange woman, and I'd never quite met anyone quite like her, though admittedly, she did remind me a little of Niala. That same feline grace. A mystery to her nature, as well. She struck me as mischievous and helpful at once, a person who rejected the idea of letting anyone get too close to her.

As the hours ticked by, I began to doubt that she could possibly have set the fire that had driven us out of Volkston.

But the truth was, I had no way of knowing.

We slept soundly until close to dawn, when I shot awake at the sound of the two horses letting out shrill whinnies of warning.

Lachlan was already on his feet, stalking toward them, his body low to the ground as he surveyed the area.

Creeping over in a crouch to press my back against the trunk of a nearby tree, I fought the frantic desire to conceal myself in my Shadow form. Something or someone was out there—I could feel a threatening presence on the air.

Worse still, I could smell the familiar, awful odor of decay and rot that so often accompanied feral Waergs on their travels.

I watched as Lachlan's head jerked up, alert and watchful. Clearly alarmed, he shifted into his wolf form, his light eyes focused on a point at the edge of the small clearing where we'd slept.

A dark form rushed out of the woods, leaping at him. In the blink of an eye, the two of them were tangled together in a horrible mess of raking claws and gnashing teeth, even as I crouched, helpless, several feet away.

Another wolf—this one light brown—rushed at the twisting bodies from the other side. Before I could even so much as react, Lachlan was on the ground, being assaulted simultaneously by two massive canines.

I leapt toward them, my blade drawn, and shouted, hoping to draw their attention. The brown wolf turned my way and snarled, but as if realizing I was no threat, turned his focus once again to his victim.

I had no choice but to do something.

I slammed my eyes shut and summoned a gleaming suit of fine chain mail that covered me from head to toe and a tall shield, light as air and transparent. Sheathing my meager dagger, I summoned a long, light sword, and charged forward, fully intending to stab one or the other assailant.

But all I could see now was mass of matted, bloody fur. It didn't help that one of Lachlan's attackers had the same color fur as his own wolf.

It was impossible to know which of them I'd be stabbing, and it wasn't a chance I was willing to take.

"Stop it!" I cried, drawing the attackers' eyes to my own. "It's not him you want, it's me! Come on!"

It was enough to get them to move away from their victim at last.

But the sight that met my eyes was horrifying.

Lachlan lay motionless on the ground, the fur around his neck soaked so thoroughly that it looked like he was wearing a collar of blood.

The two wolves began stalking toward me, their heads low, teeth bared in menacing grins.

Out of the corner of my eye, I saw more wolves coming. Two from the east, two from the west.

The only thought in my mind was that all the armor in the world wouldn't be enough to save me now.

A SUMMONING

I CLOSED MY EYES, waiting for the inevitable collision of the wolves' bodies against my own. They would barrel into me, tearing through my conjured mail, crushing my bones and reveling in my cries of agony.

You're a damned Summoner, I barked internally at myself as the pack of wild creatures closed in on me. *So summon help. Someone, anyone!*

Desperate to avoid a hideous fate, I called out for aid, though my mind was too addled, my thoughts too unfocused to cry out to any particular entity.

A moment later, even as I could smell the Waergs' foul breath on the air, a chorus of piercing screeches met my ears.

All but petrified in place, I opened my eyes and looked up to see the sky dark with winged forms descending on us.

Crows, I thought. *But...why crows?*

For some reason, the only thought that made its way into my terrified mind was the recollection that a group of them was known as a Murder.

It didn't take long to discover why that was.

The birds flew at the wolves, pecking at them even as the

monstrous creatures leapt up onto their hind legs, biting and pawing at the air.

But I could already tell it wouldn't take the wolves long to turn their attention back to me. The birds were a nuisance, but nothing they could do would be enough to vanquish such huge animals.

At best, they'd distract them for a few minutes.

Taking advantage of the temporary respite, I rushed over and grabbed the healing balm from the saddle bag on the ground, then sprinted over to Lachlan's wolf, who was groaning in pain, the whites of his eyes visible as he pulled his head up to look at me.

"Don't move," I said, rifling my way through his matted fur to apply the balm to the worst of his wounds. "I don't know if this will be enough to stop the bleeding. We're going to have to get you out of here."

When I'd applied balm to every angry gash I could see, Lachlan shifted into his human form. His neck and shoulder were bleeding from cuts that looked like they needed a series of stitches, and I wanted to scream with helplessness.

"I don't know what to do!" I told him. "The balm isn't strong enough to heal the—"

"The crows..." he said weakly, pointing to the scene behind me.

"I know, I know," I said. "They're trying their best."

"Vega...look...behind..."

I turned to see what he was talking about, expecting to find the birds had flown away and that I was about to get attacked.

But instead, my eyes landed on something entirely unexpected.

The crows were still rioting just over the wolves' heads, but from the woods, a figure had emerged. A tall, slim woman with long, sleek black hair, walking slowly toward the Waergs as if they were nothing more than a couple of alley cats in her way.

Dressed entirely in black, she held up a glove-clad hand and gestured to the beasts.

"Dasch Ellach," she said, her voice low. "Be gone."

The brown Waerg leapt over instantly and crashed into the river, which had begun to bubble and rage like it was throwing a white-water temper tantrum.

One by one, the other Waergs followed suit, leaping at the rushing river, diving in, then howling frantically as the water carried them away.

Panicked, I spun around to search for our horses, but they were nowhere to be seen, though their saddles and bridles were still tidily piled by the base of a nearby tree where we'd left them the previous night.

"What is it?" Lachlan asked weakly. "What's happened?"

"It's...nothing. It's fine," I told him, terrified that the truth might kill him. Without Dudley or Phair to carry him to the nearest town, I wasn't sure how he'd survive the next few hours.

The crows still circled overhead, forming a black vortex that looked like a perfectly synchronized cloud. But with a flick of her hand, the woman in black dispersed them, and they disappeared as quickly as they'd come.

When the strange woman had completed her task, she strode toward us, stopping a few feet away. She didn't walk so much as prowl like a mountain lion, her feet padding so lightly on the ground that I wasn't sure she left footprints in the soft earth.

Her pants were made of leather, as was her jacket. Marks that looked like a series of tiny brands decorated the jacket's sleeves—small stars and moons, I thought, though I couldn't quite tell.

Her eyes were strange and beautiful—a circle of blue around her pupil, ringed with gold, which glowed like the sun, but seemed to fade as I stared up at her. Her cheekbones were high, her jaw sculpted and exquisite.

She was as beautiful as any woman I'd ever seen.

Yet she terrified me.

"Vega Sloane," she said. "We've been waiting for your arrival. Of course, we didn't entirely expect it to happen in such... dramatic fashion. Nor so far from home."

"Who are you?" I asked, though something told me I already had some idea, at least.

"My name is Solara," she said, pulling her eyes to Lachlan. "And your friend needs aid. We must get him to my people immediately."

"Our horses..." I moaned. "They're gone."

"No matter," she said, holding a hand out. "We have no need of horses. Yours will be well on their way home by now. Come."

I grabbed what supplies I could as Solara helped Lachlan to his feet and slipped an arm around his waist to support him.

She reminded me of Mareya. The same unreadable, slightly amused expression in her eyes. The same intimidating stance.

I wondered how long it would be before she tried to kill us both.

Even so, as I stepped toward her, I let my armor fade away so that I was once again vulnerable, with nothing more than my blade to protect me. Something told me no amount of silver plate would help against an adversary such as her.

"Come," she said again, this time with a tinge of impatience. "We move on the wind."

"On the wind?" I asked. "What does *that* mean?"

"Take my hand."

I did so, even as she held onto Lachlan with the other hand.

"Close your eyes as you do to cast your own spells," she commanded. I glared at her but obeyed reluctantly, clutching her glove-covered hand hard.

"Syriah..." she murmured, then repeated the word.

A sudden gust of cold air slammed into me, and I was overcome with the immediate sensation that the forest had disappeared and we were standing on a mountaintop.

My eyes popped open to see that I was only partially wrong.

MOVING ON THE WIND

I FOUND MYSELF SURROUNDED BY...CLOUDS. Wind whipped at my face, though it didn't sting like frigid temperatures so often did. If anything, it was oddly refreshing.

"What's going on?" I asked, my voice strained as I stared into the distance. "How are we standing on nothing?"

Without a word, Solara began to walk, and I had no choice but to move with her, though I had no confidence that I wouldn't fall through the nebulous cloud under my feet.

I pulled my chin down just enough to see that far below us was a sea of forest, moving as fast as a racing train.

"What's happening?" I asked again. "Are we...flying?"

"In a manner of speaking," she told me. "In your world, there's a rumor that Witches ride brooms high in the sky. But that's not so. We don't use household items to soar through the air. We move on the wind, as I said."

"I know what you said, but...I don't understand. What are we even standing on?"

"Air," she said. "Nothing more. We are being carried to the west, because I have willed it."

I was about to lecture her on the concept of gravity, but I was convinced that if I pointed out the impossibility of our current situation, I'd suddenly go plummeting to the ground far below like a cartoon coyote.

Instead, I moved closer to Lachlan and laid a hand on his chest as we moved. "Is he going to be all right?" I asked.

He was in a state of near-collapse, leaning against Solara, his eyes half-open.

"Once he's with my Sisters, he'll be fine. It won't be long now."

I cocked my head at her, suddenly calm. "You know who I am," I said. "But how?"

The strange woman let out a laugh then—a ringing, sweet, alluring laugh that made me feel like I'd just taken a sip of something that made my head spin with intoxication.

"There are many ways to know things," she said. "Watchers. Spies. Word of mouth. But we have our own methods. I've known of you since the first day you arrived in the Otherwhere, Vega. I've known this day would come since then. And I know what you seek."

"If you know so much, maybe you can tell me why a Witch named Mareya tried to kill us two nights ago."

Solara smiled. "She did no such thing," she said. "She *did* light the fire, though."

"Right. So she set the inn we were staying in on fire, but not to kill us. I guess she just wanted to warm us up a little?"

"Two Sassers had just entered the establishment. They would have hunted you down in a matter of minutes. Mareya simply created a diversion to force them to give up, and to give you a chance at escape. She is a creature of flame...of course, you are well acquainted with one of those."

"Callum, you mean. And his dragon."

"Your Callum Drake, who dwells in the in-between." Solara spoke the words in a solemn tone that sent a chill through me. "He stands on the bridge spanning life and death. He waits to be whole again—and only one person can help him."

"I need to save him," I agreed, a hand on Lachlan's back. "I need to save them both."

"Of course. And you will have our help. You have come to the right place—or rather, I am bringing you there by invitation. You are privileged. Few humans have ever set foot in the Aradia Coven. We do not welcome those who wish to do us harm."

"I have no desire to hurt any of you. I just need to find the golden dragon. But then, you already seem to know that."

"Tell me, what will you do when you find him?"

As the wind whipped around my head, I realized how stupid my reply would sound to her.

"Speak to him, I guess," I said. "That's all I can do. Isn't it?"

Solara didn't answer me. Instead, supporting Lachlan, she stopped, turned, and pointed into the distance toward a snow-capped mountain.

"There. The peak with the jagged wall of bare stone. Its name is Sorella, and its base is our destination."

"I don't see anything down there but trees," I replied.

"Exactly."

Seconds later, we were descending rapidly, the cloud swirling around us like a maniacal tunnel of white fluff, concealing my view of the world around us.

When our descent finally decelerated to a mere crawl, Solara blew into the air and the cloud dissipated to reveal that we were standing at the center of a small, charming village. Its houses were made of wood, painted various colors: blue, green, red, white, yellow. It was the most pleasant, inviting town I'd ever laid eyes on.

In a quick motion, Solara picked Lachlan up in her arms as easily as if he'd been a bag of groceries, and began to carry him toward one of the houses—a white one, with green-painted trim and large windows overlooking the mountains.

"My home," she told me over her shoulder. "Come with me."

I followed her to the door, which opened inward as we approached, seemingly without so much as a word.

Inside, the decor was surprisingly comfortable and modern. White walls, a white sectional couch, a fireplace surrounded by clean-looking stone. A fire sprang up in its depths as we entered, rendering the place even more hospitable.

"Surprised?" Solara asked as she lay Lachlan down on the couch, not seeming to care if his substantial wounds stained the upholstery.

"A little," I admitted. "White furniture doesn't exactly scream 'Witch.'"

"*What* did you call me?" Solara snarled, straightening herself up and shooting me an angry glare.

Oh, crapburgers.

"I...I just...meant..." I stammered, my face heating.

Her expression altered into a smile, and then she laughed. "I do so enjoy doing that to visitors," she said. "I'm only teasing you...you know, to give you the impression I intend to turn you into a toad or something far worse."

Phew.

"What are you going to do with him?" I asked, trying to calm my raging heart.

Lachlan's face had gone a ghostly shade of gray-white. His wounds had stopped bleeding, but he seemed to have entered a state of delirium. He was muttering words that I couldn't make out, his eyes dull and staring at nothing in particular.

An aggressive knock sounded at the door before Solara could answer.

"Could you get that, please?" she asked. "It won't open on its own for anyone but me, I'm afraid."

I wanted to say no, but something told me I'd better just do as she said.

I jogged over and pulled the door open, only to find three women standing before me.

One was tall, with high cheekbones and dark brown, curly hair that cascaded down over her shoulders. The second was short, with bright blue eyes and deep red hair cut into a bob. And the third looked a lot like Solara. Black hair, multi-colored irises, kick-ass black clothing.

"We're here for the patient," the redhead said, barging in past me. "Where is the boy?"

"Sisters," Solara called out from the living room. "Come quickly!"

"Bloody Waergs," one of the women said. "They're such savages, what with all the biting and clawing and gnashing of teeth."

"Can you help him?" I asked, desperate and in no mood to listen to their critique of Lachlan's kind.

"Of course we can," the brown-haired woman told me with an impatient glare. "They're only nibble marks, after all."

"Then why does he look so ill?" I asked.

"Because Waergs are vile creatures with bacteria-filled mouths, that's why."

"Shh, Luna, *he's* a Waerg!" another woman chastised.

"Yes, and his mouth is full of bacteria, just like the rest of 'em." She looked down at Lachlan. "Though he's a handsome fellow. Can't say I'd resist a kiss from that one. I mean, if I were thirty years younger and, well, you know."

"Shut your pie-hole, ya crotchety old crone!" the redhead laughed. "You can yammer on about how much you want to snog him after we heal him up."

"Oh, you shut it! I was making an innocent comment! Well, *mostly* innocent." She eyed Lachlan again. "You have to admit, he's gorgeous."

"All of you, stop talking!" Solara barked. "Luna, bring me the anti-bite from the kitchen, would you?"

"Anti-bite?" I asked.

"You'll see."

The black-haired woman raced into the kitchen and came back a minute later with a bottle of some kind of blue liquid. Without wasting a second, she tipped Lachlan's head back and dribbled a few drops onto his tongue.

Meanwhile, Solara applied a balm of some sort to his wounds, though she looked puzzled as she did so.

"This salve you applied is effective," she said in an impressed tone, turning to me. "Whoever made it is highly skilled."

"That was Niala. She's a Healer," I boasted. "Best one at the Academy."

"The Academy," scoffed Merell. "She'd do better to study here, if she wants to learn the Art."

She pulled her sleeve over her hand and wiped off the salve, pulling a vial out of her pocket and pouring a generous amount of liquid on the wounds.

A billowing, slightly terrifying smoke rose up from the open gashes. Lachlan let out what sounded like a gasp, his eyes going wide, then lost consciousness.

"You could've been a little gentler," Solara scolded.

"Pfft. Rip the bandage off quick, I always say. He's out, isn't he? It's better for him."

"Yeah, passed out from the agony of it. That's some great bedside manner you have there."

I stood back, half amused, half horrified to watch the Sisters—I still wasn't sure if they were related or not—work on my good friend.

But by the time they were done, the color had returned to Lachlan's cheeks, his wounds had faded to almost nothing, and he seemed to be resting comfortably.

"Now," Solara said, turning to me. "Shall I take you on a tour of our little town?"

"I'm not sure. Should we really just leave Lachlan here? What if he wakes up?"

"The Sisters will watch him. Come, you probably need some

food, Vega. Let's go find you some. You must maintain your strength, as your journey isn't nearly done—though your friend's may be."

As my body and mind relaxed, I realized she was right. I hadn't eaten anything since the previous night. I was hungry, exhausted, and probably smelled like death, to boot.

"All right," I replied. "But I want to check in on Lachlan before too long."

"Of course. In the meantime, let's get you feeling a little more human."

LUNCH

I FOLLOWED SOLARA OUTSIDE, where she guided me down a series of broad, dirt-paved streets between houses that looked ancient and on the verge of collapse, all topsy turvy and off-kilter. Yet something about them told me there was no way they'd ever fall to pieces, like some unseen spell supported their walls with as much strength as that of stone buttresses.

"Don't worry," Solara said, reading my mind. "They look a mess to your eye, but they're quite stable. We enjoy illusion here. For those humans who do visit on occasion, we prefer not to convey power or wealth, and prefer to discourage outsiders from staying too long. So our houses tend to morph into something decrepit-looking when a visitor is around. I suppose it's the equivalent of a lizard whose scales are bright yellow or red, to warn off any potential predators."

It made sense, in a strange kind of way.

"Where are we going?" I asked, nervous and excited at once. Everything that had occurred since I'd first met Solara had been surreal. The cloud-walking, or wind-walking, or whatever it was. Her strange companions who bickered like spouses but could work miracles.

And Solara herself, who was the most self-assured, interesting woman I'd ever met. I couldn't help wondering if I'd ever have half her confidence.

"I'm taking you downtown, inasmuch as we actually have a downtown. We'll eat a little, and talk. You need a plan of action, Vega. You have some difficult days ahead."

"Can you see the future?" I asked. "Do you know what's going to happen?"

"Not exactly. But you're not the first person ever to hope to reconnect a dragon with its human, you know."

"Wait—I'm not?" I was stunned. "Merriwether led me to believe I was."

"That's probably because no one has ever *succeeded* at it before. Which is a different thing."

"Do you think there's a chance that I could succeed?"

"No," Solara said without hesitation.

My heart sank. "Well, that was fast."

"I didn't finish," she said as we walked past leaded glass windows and brightly-painted doors. "I don't think you can do what you're hoping to do. You can't turn back time and make the dragon shifter what he once was. But I *do* think you can save Callum. I will say nothing more, however, as I don't want to create a self-fulfilling prophecy that leads you to fail."

"Can't you give me some advice or something?"

Solara stopped walking and turned to face me. "Sure. I advise you to seek out the dragon and see what happens. If that fails, come back to me."

"It won't fail. *I* won't fail."

"Good. Keep that positivity with you. You'll need it when you're racked with doubt."

With that cheery message, we continued our walk in silence.

We stopped at a small house tucked between two shops. Solara pushed the door open to the tinkling of bells, and gestured me to head in.

When I did, the scent of fresh-baked bread met my nose, and I was immediately transported to my grandmother's kitchen.

"Maeve?" Solara called out when she'd stepped inside.

A young woman with two tidy blond braids came out of a side room into the foyer and smiled when she saw us.

"Stew today," she said. "Just finished. You're right on time."

"Wonderful," Solara replied, following the other woman into a small, cozy kitchen. I went in after her, and Maeve seated us both at a small bistro table by a large window that looked out onto the street.

"This town..." I said, "it's so peaceful. So quiet. I feel weirdly relaxed."

It was true. Despite Lachlan's injuries, and the fact that Callum was still at home in a coma, I felt like my worries had slipped out of my mind and run a million miles away. I wanted little more than to sit in this kitchen for days on end, to smell fresh baking and savory cooking, and ask Solara questions about what it was like to live in such a place.

"We strive for a calm environment," she told me as Maeve brought over a fresh, sliced loaf of bread with a side of soft butter. The bread was steaming, and as I slathered butter on a piece, my mouth watered. "We deal with enough stress in our lives. This is our own private Utopia."

"Stress?" I asked through a mouthful of bread. "Why?"

Solara pushed out a sigh. "To be a Witch is to be at constant war. War against men who wish us dead. Against enemies who wish to take our powers from us. Against those who want to steal our land for themselves."

"You're saying people actually attack the town?"

Solara shook her head. "Most can't find it, so attack is all but an impossibility. It's when we venture out of our town limits that we find ourselves in danger. It's why Witches have evolved over centuries to master the art of Healing, of concealment, of combat via magical means. Of…flying." Her lips twitched into a playful smile with the last word.

"You're basically wizards," I said.

"Yes, we are. *Witch* was never meant to be a derogatory term. It only ended up that way because humans harnessed the power of the word to condemn us, whereas they created a mythology around wizards that paints them as benevolent entities. When the truth is, there are as many cruel wizards as there are cruel Witches."

"You say humans harnessed the power of the word," I pointed out, taking another bite of bread. "But I think you mean *men*."

Solara shook her head. "Many of those who despise us are men who resent our powers. But some women hate us, as well."

"Why?"

She shrugged and turned to our hostess. "Maeve, what's your thinking?"

"My thinking is that women don't like when we show up in town and charm all the young, handsome men into coming to bed with us. Sometimes, the young women, too."

With that, she let out a full-on belly laugh.

"Are there any men here, in Aradia?" I asked, not sure if I should join in on the mirth.

"None," Solara said. "We like to keep it that way. If one of our Sisters wishes to find a man, she may do so, of course. It's not uncommon that one of us heads to Domburg—that's the nearest town—and finds herself a *friend* for the evening."

"But Witches don't ever get married?"

"Oh, yes. Some do. They must leave the Coven to do so, however. We are not a society of families. We're a society of women, and we prefer to keep our secrets to ourselves."

"But Lachlan is here—at your house. He's a man. I mean, basically."

"He's the first man who's been invited past our borders in quite some time," Solara said. "And only because he needed our help—and because he was your protector. He is, of course, welcome, despite the fact that he has a wolf inside him. We know his heart. We know whose side he's on."

"Thank you," I said. "He's a good person. He's saved me more than a few times."

"And you care deeply about him."

My cheeks flushed feverishly hot. I thought about denying it, but something told me Solara would see right through the lie. "I care about him," I said. "But he's not the one I love."

Solara reached an elegant hand out and took my own. "You can love more than one person," she said. "Love is complicated. It's unnerving and hostile and warm, all at once. Your heart opening itself to Lachlan does not mean you're betraying Callum. All it means is that you have a big heart."

"But I would never do anything—I'd never kiss Lachlan or—"

"No, of course not. But count yourself lucky that two men adore you enough to be willing to sacrifice their very lives for you. It's more than most women ever get to experience in an entire lifetime."

I half-smiled then, but quickly erased the expression from my face. The truth was, it felt wretched to think I could be hurting Lachlan. Leading him on by my mere presence, by our closeness, by my reliance on him.

"I should continue alone," I said. "I should leave him here to heal, and go find the dragon. It's not fair to bring him with me, especially after what's happened."

"Yes. You alone should seek out Caffall," Solara murmured.

I nodded. "Do you know where he is?"

"He's been seen to the northwest. There is a town up there—a town of fishermen and hunters. Grell and Waergs, with a few humans thrown in for good measure. They say Caffall has been tormenting the population. Burning houses to the ground. The fear is that he has a taste for it now—for destruction and mayhem. They worry that the entire town will be destroyed, and the livelihoods of the families there along with it."

"I need to talk to Caffall," I said. "To stop him."

Solara smirked. "You really think you can reason with a dragon," she scoffed. "I must say, I admire you for it."

"I don't know, but shouldn't I try?"

"Of course you should. And you have my blessing. As I said, it's what you must do if you wish to save your Callum."

When we'd finished eating, Solara thanked Maeve, rose to her feet and gestured for me to follow her out the door.

Outside, she turned to the right and pointed into the distance. "That way, if you follow the road for three hours or so, is the town of La Baie," she said. "You will have no choice but to pass through it if you wish to find Caffall. It is not a friendly place. They are hostile and defensive at the best of times, but with the dragon flying overhead on a near-daily basis, they grow even more angry and wary of strangers. But it's where you'll need to go if you want to find answers. I suggest that you stay here tonight, and set off first thing tomorrow. From the looks of it, you need a good night's sleep and a couple of proper meals. I'll see to it that you receive both—and perhaps some fresh clothing."

"Thank you—again," I said. But when I set my jaw and stared into the distance, Solara asked what was on my mind.

"What if I can't persuade him?" I asked. "What if Caffall has no desire to help?"

Solara reached for my shoulder. Her hand was gentle but firm.

"You will find a way, Vega. Of that, I am certain. It may not be the way you expect—and you may have a difficult decision to make. But like others, I've seen enough of the future to have pictured Callum fighting for his place on the throne of the Otherwhere. I am never wrong about these things. And prophecies always come to pass, in some way or other."

"The prophecy," I said, spinning to face her with a jolt of hopeful energy. "You really believe it will come true?"

With a sad smile, she nodded. "It has already begun to come true—at least, the most disastrous part of the prediction. Our job is to ensure that the rest comes true, as well. Be careful, and be strong. In the morning, I'll help you find your way to La Baie. For tonight, though, I want you to relax and forget your troubles."

LEAVING

When Solara and I returned to her house, Lachlan was nowhere to be seen, and the pristine white sectional had returned to its former glory.

"Where is he?" I asked, terrified that something horrible had happened.

"In the Healer's Haven," Solara assured me as she removed her black leather jacket to reveal a translucent black sweater that hugged every curve like a glove. I hadn't thought it was possible, but now she looked even *more* impossibly confident than before. "He'll be resting and somewhat sedated until his wounds are fully healed. It's the safest path for him."

She showed me to my bedroom—a large, beautiful chamber with a wall of windows at the far end that looked out to the mountain peaks in the distance. I felt like I'd walked into a chalet in Colorado after a day of downhill skiing.

On the bed—a queen-sized, white linen-coated luxury item—was a set of clothing. Black pants, similar to Solara's. A black tank top and black sweater with bell sleeves and an open neck, as well as some undergarments.

"You're really willing to lend me these?" I asked, feeling the soft leather of the pants.

"You can keep them," she laughed, "provided you succeed. Hell, keep them even if you don't. One day soon, however, I suspect you'll learn to summon your own clothing."

"I already can," I said in a slightly sheepish tone. "But it disappears after a while, when the spell breaks."

"It doesn't need to, you know. You underestimate your powers, I'm afraid. Perhaps as you grow into them, you'll learn just how skilled you really are."

"I hope so," I gushed, turning her way to see that she was smiling at me. "I really don't know how to express my gratitude for everything you and the others have done for us."

"Don't thank me yet. Our work isn't done." She looked over at the bed. "Now, why don't you have a nap? I'll send up some food when the time comes. Your top priority at the moment should be sleep. You'll need your wits about you tomorrow."

A sudden heaviness overtook me then, like she'd drugged me with her words. As she scooped the clothing off the bed and laid it over a nearby chair, I nodded, crawled under the covers, and closed my eyes.

I DIDN'T WAKE up until dawn the following morning, when I discovered a tray on the night stand next to the bed, covered with a delicious assortment of food. Oatmeal, fresh fruit, hot coffee in a pot, juice, eggs. Everything I could possibly want.

After I'd eaten, showered in the adjacent bathroom that I hadn't even noticed the night before, and changed into the clothing Solara had supplied, I raced downstairs only to find the house empty.

A note sat on the kitchen table:

To reach the Healer's Haven, turn right out the front door and proceed past the town square until you see the yellow house with purple trim. You'll find Lachlan there.

I strode quickly down the street, eager to see him, and when I reached the house described in the note, the door opened inward as if it had been awaiting my arrival.

Lachlan was in the first room to the right of the front hall, and I raced in to stand at his bedside.

As I approached, his eyes opened.

The color had returned to his cheeks, and his eyes had brightened. He was dressed in a soft-looking blue cotton tunic that brought out the green in his eyes.

He smiled when he saw me.

"I was wondering when I'd see your face again," he said as I sat down on the edge of the bed. "I'm sorry if I gave you a scare."

"You did, but there's nothing to be sorry about. You keep getting injured to protect me." I reached out a hand and took his for a second, squeezing before letting go again. "I can't let you keep doing that. It's not right."

"It's what I vowed to do, Vega," he said. "I can't exactly say it's my pleasure, but it's certainly not a burden."

"Still, you've looked out for me for so long," I said. "You need to rest and recover, and you should do that here. We've come a long way, but I'll do the rest on my own."

Lachlan started to protest, but I held a hand up. "Nope. I'm not going to fight with you about this. Solara is bringing me to a town up north where they've spotted Caffall. The residents can point me to him. I'll be fine, I promise."

"Vega, you won't be safe on your own. We're talking about the Northwest. The land known as Dragonhelm. The people who live up there, they probably carry weapons everywhere they go—or worse, they're *walking* weapons, themselves. A stranger walks into town, and they might kill on sight. Even if that stranger is a woman—" he eyed me for a moment, "—dressed like you are. Actually, *especially* a woman dressed like you. You look like—"

"A Witch?" I asked.

"Well, yeah."

"I'm okay with that," I replied with more pride than I would have confessed. "Besides, if they kill me, I guess you'll get to avenge my death." I winked at him, and when he scowled, I punched his arm gently. "Just relax, would you? I've got this."

"I think the mountain air is making you loopy. You're about to embark on the most dangerous leg of this mission of yours."

You're just jealous that you don't get to come freeze your butt off with me."

"Maybe a little. But I also care about you. I don't want to see you hurt."

"Yes, you've made that abundantly clear by repeatedly encouraging Waergs to tear into *your* flesh instead of mine. This is my way of saying 'Stop it.'"

"I'm serious."

"So am I. Look—I'm near the end here. If I have to, I'll use my spells. Don't forget, I can disappear almost completely. I can protect myself indefinitely, if I have to. But more importantly…" I lowered my chin and my voice. "More importantly, I think this is something I need to do alone. For some reason, I don't think Caffall would like it if I showed up with you."

Lachlan looked taken aback. "You think the dragon might be jealous?"

"I don't know. Maybe. It's hard to explain. He and I—I feel like we have a strange kind of bond. Like he's part of Callum, but he's not. I've looked into his eyes. I've felt something from him, like there's, I don't know, a mutual respect between us. I don't want to do anything that might set him off."

"Like bring a Waerg with you. Because he might think you actually care about me."

"He's a dragon, Lachlan. I'm not sure his thought process is as sophisticated as all that. It's more that he might think my loyalties aren't clear."

"You might be surprised at how deeply dragons and wolves can feel, Vega."

I chewed on my lip for a second before nodding. "You're right. I'm sorry. I have no idea what it feels like to be you—or the wolf inside you. So tell me—does your wolf feel love?"

Lachlan looked at me then with an intensity that I'd rarely seen in his eyes. "He feels enough love that he would willingly give his life to protect someone he cares about."

I pulled my eyes away, my chest tightening. "Of course," I said. "I suppose that's what a pack is. Loyal wolves, looking out for each other."

He reached a hand out and wrapped his fingers around my forearm. "That's not what I meant, and you know it."

I leapt to my feet, pulling away from his grip. "You can't say things like that," I said, suddenly near tears. "You can't talk to me about love and affection and loyalty. Please—just don't. You know I can't reciprocate your feelings."

"I think you *do* feel something for me," he said. "I'm sure you do, in fact."

"That's not fair. Of course I feel something for you. We've spent days together. You keep saving my life. You're one of my best friends. How could I not feel something?"

"Friends," he said bitterly, like he'd grown to hate the word even more over the days we'd spent together.

"Friends," I replied. "That's all we can ever be. Please, if you care about me even a little bit, don't ask me for more."

With that, I left him and went to find Solara.

I needed to leave this place.

And the sooner, the better.

TO LA BAIE

I FOUND Solara waiting for me just outside her house, staring out toward the mountains.

"There you are," she said without turning my way. "Everything all right?"

"Fine," I said, trying hard to keep my voice even after my moment of tension with Lachlan. "Just fine."

"Good."

She led me inside and opened a closet to one side of the living room, only to pull out my pack. "We've filled it with food and other supplies," she said. "Some, you will need. Others, I hope you don't. Keep your cloak on, your hood up. Only use your powers if you must. Don't hesitate to use them if you're in danger. Now come—we have a cloud to catch."

When we were outside again, Solara escorted me to the small town square down the street from her house. At its center was what looked like a stone obelisk, carved with the shapes of all sorts of animals and other creatures. "Ready?" she asked.

I nodded. "Ready."

Shooting one final look toward the Healer's Haven a few doors down, I took her hand.

I could see Lachlan's silhouette framed in his window as he stood staring at me. As I watched, he pressed a hand to the glass.

I wanted to wave, but I couldn't. I was numb inside, my emotions in a deep freeze. If my friendship wasn't enough for him, we would have to sever all ties. There would be no cordial waving or friendly smiles.

It was for his own good.

At least, that was what I told myself.

The ugly truth was, it was for *mine*.

"Off we go," Solara said, pretending not to notice the silent exchange.

A second later, we were shooting skyward as if standing in the fastest express elevator in the history of the world. Only I didn't feel any sense of nausea or terror—only the sense that our elevation was changing, and it made perfect sense.

Seconds later, I found myself once again surrounded by a sea of cloud high above the mountains. The air was warm, and I could breathe normally, despite telling myself that I should be suffocating.

We began to walk north-west, following a dense path of mist that revealed itself little by little in front of us. And as we advanced, the landscape below moved rapidly, and once again, it seemed like we were stationary while the earth was shifting at a fast clip beneath us.

"We'll be there in no time," Solara assured me. "A few minutes. I will leave you on your own, to make your way into town."

"You can't come with me?" I asked.

"La Baie is not friendly to my kind. But you should be fine."

"Lachlan said I looked like a Witch," I told her. "They might try to kick me out the second they set eyes on me."

A sense of dread had begun to creep its way through my mind and body. It was the first time I'd ventured out on my own on such a dangerous mission since I'd gone to Uldrach to rescue Will and Liv from the queen's dungeons.

And that particular mission hadn't exactly gone smoothly.

"Trust me—they won't see you as a Witch, but as something else. Something that attracts and confuses them at once," Solara advised me. "Make use of the coin Merriwether gave you. Ask questions. Reward those who answer. But don't flaunt your wealth, or you'll be pursued. If you must stay in town, make sure you keep your whereabouts as private as possible. And like I said, keep an eye out for allies."

"You really think I'll have some in this place?"

"I can't say. But the Academy has a broad reach—every corner of the Otherwhere has Merriwether's Rangers on high alert. You may discover you're not alone in your desire to saving Callum Drake. But I warn you—there are others who would love to see him ended. The queen...."

I nodded. "Wants him dead, as well as me. Of course, that's nothing new."

"Welcome to the world of Witches," Solara said with a laugh. "People have been hanging our kind for generations for little more than our existence."

"I thought they burned you at the stake," I shot out without thinking, only to notice an amused grin on her lips. "Sorry. It's just what I heard."

"Nope. Hanging is the preferred method of killing us. I suppose some felt that burning us would release our toxins into the air, whereas a noose was a nice clean end."

"You're really getting me excited about this little trip of mine, you know," I said with a nervous laugh. "So many ways I could end up dead."

"Don't worry. Where you're going, they're far more likely to stab you or shoot you with an arrow than hang you."

"Great."

As Solara had promised, we began our descent after a few minutes. It was as if we were slipping down a rapidly moving escalator, except for the fact that our feet floated seemingly in mid-air as we neared the earth.

We landed on a patch of damp grass next to a dirt road. A forest surrounded us, dense with mature pine trees.

Solara pointed ahead. "Follow the road," she said, "and you'll come to La Baie. Find a pub—the Otherwhere's more potent ales are very good at loosening tongues. Get anyone who looks useful to talk to you. Use your charms, if necessary."

"Charms?" I asked, flustered.

Solara looked genuinely surprised for the first time since I'd met her. "You're a beautiful young woman, Vega. Surely you know what I'm talking about."

"You mean, like, flirting?"

Solara laughed. "Youth really is wasted on the young," she said. "Yes. Flirting. Flatter the men. Tell them how impressive they are. Pull them close and make them feel special. Then extract every ounce of information you can."

The thought of getting close to anyone but Callum—or Lachlan, if I was being honest with myself—horrified me.

"My mother used to say, 'You catch more flies with honey than with vinegar,'" I replied. "I assume that's what you're talking about."

"Precisely. A woman is a powerful entity. We may not have the brute strength of men, but we can bend most of them to our will with little more than a smile. Don't forget that the most effective weapons in your arsenal require little to no magic. It's a sad truth, but it's nevertheless true."

"I'm not sure I really want to go around flirting with strange men."

"Of course you don't. Neither do I. But it's saved me more than once, and it's been a miraculous way to obtain free goods and services."

Now I couldn't help but laugh. Solara had a disarming way of confessing exactly who and what she was with no shame, no self-consciousness. She was a Witch. She was a woman who dressed in form-fitting black leather, and she knew exactly the effect her appearance had on those around her.

I had to respect her for it.

"Now, go," she said, looking toward the town. "Keep your head low and your eyes on everyone around you. Don't let your guard down for a minute. Find the dragon. After that, it's anyone's guess what will happen."

"What's going to happen to Lachlan?" I asked. "How will he get home?"

"We'll make sure he gets to the Academy when the time is right. But right now, he needs to heal...in more ways than one."

"You think I was cruel to him," I said.

"I don't know anything about your personal business. All I know is that he's a young man who suffers from a certain sort of pain—but one that will go away with time. It isn't your duty to ensure his happiness."

"But I don't want to cause his sadness, either."

"Unfortunately, sometimes one can't help but break a heart to preserve one's own."

With a quick, surprising hug, Solara backed away. "I won't keep you any longer, or we run the risk of being seen together on this road. If they spot you with me, your chances of finding help will be slim to none."

With one final goodbye, she shot into the sky so fast that I hardly saw her go. I looked up, only to see a new bank of clouds rolling into the blue high above me, then disappearing quickly in a gust of wind headed to the south.

I was alone now, with nothing but my flawed instincts to guide me.

THE GRELL AND GRIMESTONE

I PULLED my hood up as I began the walk toward the small town of La Baie.

Smoke billowed from a series of chimneys that topped the rows of small wooden houses lining the streets. I wasn't sure if I was only imagining the damp, penetrating cold setting into my bones as I hiked along, or the menacing gray of the sky, which only seemed to darken the closer I came to the town's border.

I didn't quite feel like I was in the Otherwhere anymore. It was as if the sense of magic and wonder I'd grown accustomed to in this land had been replaced by a vague feeling of hostility—a low, threatening growl manifested by the town itself.

Tense with a feeling of vulnerability that came with Lachlan's absence, I forged ahead, keeping my eyes on the road, which seemed to narrow as it wove between the structures to either side.

As I stepped into the town, I pulled the cloak tighter around myself, one hand pressed to the pack that was slung over my right shoulder. Shadows began appearing on doorsteps, eyeing me with scrutiny in spite of the cloak that should have masked my presence at least a little.

A curly-haired woman sneering to my left. A Grell, eyeing me through golden irises to my right, his nostrils flaring.

I'd walked a few blocks along the dirt road when a cart came up beside me, pulled by what looked like two massive oxen…only they weren't entirely like any animal I'd ever seen before. They were furry, like shaggy sheepdogs, and instead of hooves, they had large paws with long claws. Their heads and bodies, though, were shaped like those of the large cattle I'd seen in my world.

I was beginning to wonder how many species existed in the Otherwhere that I didn't even begin to know about.

I walked along street after street until I found what seemed to be the main drag—a wide, cobblestone road with shops to either side, each selling fish, meat, or hunting and fishing gear. Occasionally I'd pass a sign for a clothing shop, but when I peered, intrigued, at the window displays, all the goods for sale looked as though they had been worn for decades before being put on sale.

The town was devoid of color or joy. It was a sepia world of brown and gray, as if La Baie had long since given up on the idea of looking like anything other than a mud-soaked, weathered old boot.

When I finally came to what looked like a small grocery store, I stepped inside, if only to warm myself up a little.

A short, squat woman with a small set of curling horns stood on the other side of the counter. She eyed me curiously, and I looked at her only long enough to note that her pupils were shaped like horizontal black streaks rather than circles.

"Can I help ya, stranger?" she asked, leaning one bony elbow on the counter.

"I'm just looking, thanks," I replied. When she grunted something unintelligible, I picked up a small bag of what looked like beef jerky and brought it over to her. "Actually, I'll buy this," I said. "And could you tell me where the nearest pub is, please?"

She nodded toward the door. "Keep walking up the road.

Can't miss the Grell and Grimestone. It'll be on your right. Watch yourself, though. The clientele can be…lively."

"Lively?" I asked.

"Eh, there's not much goes on around here, so the male folk like to start fights. Brawls over nothing. Fisticuffs. It's their favorite pastime, really."

"I see."

"Though in recent days, of course, they've calmed down a bit, what with them *Ormyr* showing their faces round these parts."

"Ormyr?"

"Dragon Hunters," she said, sending a chill trickling its way down my spine. "*They* stay sober, those ones. Can shoot anything from a mile away. They're after the golden beast, of course." She narrowed her eyes at me. "I'm assuming that's why you're here, too. No girl with your looks'd show up in La Baie without having a damned good reason."

"I don't know anything about a golden beast," I replied, my voice tight as I set a couple of gold coins on the counter. "And I'd appreciate it if you forgot you saw me."

"Lips are sealed," she replied, feigning zipping her mouth shut with one hand as she grabbed the coins and pocketed them. "Just watch yourself. Tell anyone you talk to you're looking for work, if you must say anything at all. Don't reveal anything about where you come from—if you're from where I think."

I nodded and turned away, taking the bag of jerky with me. I wanted to ask her where she thought I was from, but something told me it would be best not to know.

I made my way along the street until I came to the Grell and Grimestone, a seedy-looking pub with leaded, warped glass windows and a rickety, cracked sign that squeaked back and forth in the wind like it was either beckoning me in or warning me off.

When I pushed the door open, the combined stench of fish,

sweat, and ale smacked me in the face in an aggressive series of punches.

I tried my best not to wince with disgust as I headed for a stool by the bar and seated myself. Eyes seemed to lock themselves on me from every dark corner, though I suspected it was my scent rather than my appearance that drew them.

Assessing, wondering, guessing.

"What can I get you?" asked the bartender, making his way over to stand in front of me. I looked up to see a pair of green-gray eyes that glinted in the darkness.

A Waerg.

Hopefully he was one of the nice ones.

"Whatever your local ale is," I said, straightening my spine in the hopes of appearing confident, not to mention older than my seventeen years.

The man looked me up and down, nodded, and proceeded to grab a glass.

"You must be one of the new girls," he said as he handed me the drink.

"New girls?"

"You know. To replace the ones ol' Varney lost when the beast came down from the cliff." He shook his head. "Of all the domiciles the dragon could've targeted, he went after the Steward's house. Just amazing."

"The Steward?" I asked, feeling stupid for echoing everything the man said.

"The Steward of the Northwest. The land beyond the mountains has always had a leader of sorts—someone to keep things in order, you know. Ol' Varney has been in charge for some time. But, well, you probably know what happened."

"I really don't."

"They say it was a cardiac incident. He fled the scene, you know, when the dragon came. Watched the place burn to the ground. A pity, really—it was full of art and trinkets. Old family heirlooms, they say. That's why he lost his servant girls. They ran away, said there was no point in sticking around when there was no longer a house to clean and whatnot. But you're smart—you know perfectly well there's plenty of cleanup to be done."

"The Steward—yes, I remember now," I lied. "I'd forgotten that's his title. How is he doing?"

The bartender shrugged. "It's impossible to say if he'll survive the next few days. He's on the old side, and he's…enjoyed life, if you catch my drift. Not the healthiest of Grells. Anyhow, they've moved him to a new house, and he'll soon be looking for new staff, so you're in luck, if that's why you've come. I suppose he's hoping to give the impression that all is well and normal."

"This dragon," I said, trying to appear mildly disinterested, "do you think he'll come back?"

"Probably. He's been terrorizing us the last few nights. He flies over the town, wreaking absolute havoc. He could probably burn the whole place to the ground in one fell swoop, but it seems he's biding his time. Amusing himself. He goes for one or two houses at a time, like it's a game or something."

"Or maybe he's drawing attention to himself in a cry for help," I said under my breath.

"What's that?"

"Nothing. Hey—um—do you know where he is now?"

"Why?" the bartender laughed. "You looking to go tame him into submission?"

I shrugged and offered up an innocent grin. "Just curious, I suppose."

"They say he's in a cave up by the Blancs. The White Cliffs, that is. Nothing but snow and ice up there. Not a very hospitable place. It's probably why he likes to come down and set fires—to warm himself up. Shame he doesn't bring marshmallows with him."

"I see."

"Well, let me know if there's anything else you'd like," the man said, shooting me a final bemused look before moving away. "And good luck to you."

"Thanks."

I'd just taken a first sip of my ale when I felt someone sit down to my right. Instinctively, I pulled my hood around my face, hoping to conceal my features.

After a few seconds of merciful silence, I allowed myself a quiet exhalation.

But my relief was cut short when a deep voice said, "You might want to think twice before asking any more questions about dragons."

THE RANGER

I FROZE, set my glass down, and said, "Oh? Why's that?"

"People might figure out that you're here for something other than a housekeeping job."

"I'm just curious," I said, turning the stranger's way to see a young man in a red tunic, a quiver strapped to his back with elegantly fletched arrows on full display.

I found myself examining him more intently than I should have. I didn't recognize him, but there was no mistaking the distinct crimson of that tunic. I'd seen it a thousand times.

"See something you like?" he asked with a grin.

He was interesting. Not exactly handsome, but appealing nonetheless, in a rugged, weathered sort of way. He could have been anywhere from eighteen to thirty; it was hard to see past a layer of thick stubble and a series of scars that told me he'd probably scrapped with more than one Waerg in his lifetime. His eyes were hazel like mine, his skin pale, and his lashes were dark and thick.

"Have you ever been to the Academy for the Blood-Born?" I asked in a whisper.

"Yes," he breathed back, leaning toward me with a half-smile on his lips. "And if you had any sense whatsoever, you wouldn't mention its name around here."

With that, he straightened up as someone pulled up a stool to my left.

"Buy you a drink, Beauty?" a gruff voice asked. I twisted around to see a massive, red-faced, bearded man in a leather jacket eyeing me. "C'mon, leave this weaselly dragon-hunting Ranger and spend some time with a *proper* man."

"I'm fine where I am, thanks," I said with as charming a smile as I could muster.

The man took my rejection as an invitation to grab my arm and try to forcibly yank me off my stool so hard that I nearly went crashing to the ground.

In a moment of panicked instinct, I called on my Shadow form and vanished, retreating from his grip and sprinting over to the far corner of the pub, my heart racing so fast I was sure it could be heard over the din of the pub's loudest talkers.

"Oh, crap," I said under my breath, wondering if I should flee the scene entirely.

The man who'd grabbed me looked around, puzzled. "What is this?" he asked. "Witches aren't allowed in this town!"

The Ranger rose to his feet and put a hand on the other man's shoulder. "She's not a Witch," he said. "You're just drunk. You blanked out. She walked away. And now, you're confused."

"I'm not!"

"No? How many fingers am I holding up, then?" the Ranger asked, unsheathing a razor-sharp dagger from his leather baldric and holding it in front of the other man's face.

"Enough!" the bartender shouted, venturing over to break up the altercation. "Quinn, go back to your table. Stop harassing my customers. And *you*—no knives in my establishment, unless you're using 'em to cut into a slab of venison."

"Fair enough," my protector said as the man called Quinn staggered over to a table by the wall, mumbling to himself.

"You can come back now," the Ranger mouthed quietly, staring in my direction. "No one's watching."

I pulled myself out of Shadow form and headed over, seating myself next to him once again. "Thanks for that," I told him. "I didn't mean to disappear. It was just a moment of…"

"Don't be sorry," he interrupted. "It's a good trick you've got there, Vega."

I shook my head, looked down at my hands, and laughed. "How does everyone in this entire land know my name?"

"There aren't a lot of Shadows in our world," he said. "Very few have *ever* existed, in fact. It's not exactly hard for an ex-student of the Academy to guess who you are." He sipped his beer. "The people in this town think I'm an Ormyr—that I'm here to find the dragon—but the truth is, I've been looking for *you*."

"What? How did you know I'd be here?"

"I didn't," he said with a shrug. "But Merriwether sent me anyhow. That is, he sent word that the Rangers of the Northwest were to keep an eye out for you. I know what you're looking to do, and it's my job to make sure you're protected while you do it. Though I didn't entirely expect you to be alone. I thought you were with a Waerg?"

"I was. He…was injured. He's staying with friends."

"I see."

"Anyhow, I can protect myself," I protested.

"Of course you can. Just flit away into the shadows, right?"

"I can do other things, as well," I said.

"I'm sure you can." He looked my way with an amused look that half-irritated and half-charmed me. "My name's Aithan," he said. "I'm a friend of Crow's."

On hearing the name of one of my friends from the Academy, I actually managed to relax. "Crow!" I exclaimed. "How is he doing?"

"I think he's all right. You've probably seen him more recently than I have, truth be told. I heard about the retrieval of the Lyre.

I'm sorry for what happened there—with Lord Drake and his dragon. As you know by now, the people of this town are paying dearly for it."

"You call Callum 'Lord Drake?'"

"Would you rather I called him King?" he asked.

"I'm just surprised. I didn't realize the Rangers knew who and what he was."

"The younger ones may not. But I've been around for some time," Aithan said. "I was there when his sinister sister took the throne. I've known his secret for years now. Some of the other Rangers know, as well."

"Wait—you look like you're maybe twenty years old," I replied. "How many years are we talking about?"

"Your Callum looks young, too, but I suspect you know he's not," Aithan replied.

"Sure, but…he's…" I stopped myself and eyed the man in red. "You're a shifter of some sort?"

"Hawk," he said with a nod, and for the first time, I saw his eyes flash with a brightness I hadn't noticed earlier. "As you know, we don't age like some do. We're affected little by the passage of time. Of course, I'm no dragon shifter. They may as well be immortal. Unless…"

"Unless something causes the Severing," I said bitterly. "Anyhow, you're lucky that age doesn't affect you much. I'm envious."

"In some ways we are fortunate, yes," he said. "But it also means we tend to live drawn-out lives. Many of us spend decades alone, in the service of the Academy or some other place. Don't get me wrong—I fully support Merriwether and his cause. But at times, this life of ours is a lonely one."

"Are there a lot of Rangers up here?" I asked.

"No. There are a few allies, of course. A few Grells here in town have long been eyes and ears for the Academy—it's how I heard you were seen making your way into town. But there are enemies about, as well. Which is why you should come with me when we're done with our drinks."

"Where will you take me?" I asked, tightening.

"To a cabin on the way to the White Cliffs," he said. "Don't worry so much, Vega. I wouldn't touch a hair on the head of Merriwether's flesh and blood."

"Wait—you know he's my grandfather, too?"

This guy was like a master sleuth. I couldn't help feeling impressed, horrified though I was by his vast knowledge of my background.

Aithan nodded. "Even if I didn't, I'd know Mariah Sloane's granddaughter anywhere. You and she aren't entirely alike, of course, but you have the same glint in your eye that she did. I'll never forget her, showing up to the Otherwhere with each Relic, like she'd conquered the world."

"You knew her?"

"We were at the Academy together. I can't say I was particularly kind to her—the Zerkers have a long tradition..."

"Of being asses to the Seekers. I'm well aware."

"Don't take it personally. We tend to have a lot of youthful energy and no idea how to rid ourselves of it. It tends to manifest itself in bouts of rage. But we're a harmless bunch, really."

"Tell that to all the bruises and near-death experiences I suffered at Zerkers' hands when I was in my combat classes."

Aithan laughed. "Glad to hear the tradition continues. Well, it seems they toughened you up, at least."

My brows knitted together. "I toughened *myself* up, thank you very much."

"Clearly. I can't imagine even Mariah Sloane herself venturing this far north on a fool's errand."

"You think it's a fool's errand? Looking for Caffall?"

"*Looking?* Nah. I think you're a fool if you want to confront him, however. Whatever notions you may have in that very pretty head of yours about him, you'll find him changed. He's not part of Lord Drake anymore; he's a wild animal. Picture a rabid Aegis Cat who can breathe fire, only without the warmth or charm."

"I'll talk to him," I said. "I'll remind him what he's missing. He needs Callum, just like Callum needs him. They're not complete without each other."

"I'm afraid that's where you're wrong." Aithan sipped his beer, his eyes veering around the pub as if to see if anyone was close enough to listen in.

"What do you mean?"

"Shifters' human sides are weak," he said. "Far weaker than the beasts inside us. I'm not telling you this to disparage Callum—he's a good man. A great man, even. It's not weakness that makes humans succumb to the Severing when our animals are stolen from us. It's our cursed humanity. We cling to the part of ourselves that made us whole, and when it's ripped away—when all we're left with is the human form, which feels to a shifter like a soulless prison—we wilt and shrivel inside. Meanwhile, the wild creature who once resided inside us escapes, liberated from its former shackles. For the beast, it is a release and a relief."

"So you think Caffall will be too attached to the idea of his freedom to want to return to Callum."

"I don't know what he might want. But in any case, a shifter, once torn apart, does not simply reunite its two halves." He took a large swig of his drink and turned my way. His tone altered when he said, "Look, I'm sorry, Vega. I will do what I can to help you, but I don't want to give you false hope. Even if you could speak to Caffall, and even if he listened to you as I'm listening now—even if you convinced him that the best thing for him was to return to Callum—they would still remain two separate entities. You can't stitch them back together."

"You're saying there's no hope," I replied, surprised that I managed to speak the words so matter-of-factly. "I refuse to believe that. Merriwether and Callum always talk about fate.

Always. There's a prophecy that says Callum will end up on the throne. You call him *Lord*, for God's sake. We all feel it—we all *know* who he's meant to be. Which means there has to be a way to save him, no matter what you say."

"Maybe there is," Aithan replied, his face softening with sympathy. "All I'm saying is that it may not happen the way you're hoping it will."

THE CABIN IN THE WOODS

AITHAN'S HORSE was grazing in a nearby field when we reached the edge of town. Tall and dapple gray, his mane cascaded down his neck in gentle white waves.

"What's his name?" I asked, stroking the gelding's neck.

"Tyrannus," Aithan replied. "Tyr, for short."

"Seriously? He's so beautiful—such a hostile-sounding name doesn't seem to suit him."

"He was a holy terror as a colt," Aithan assured me. "He's settled down quite a lot."

"Good to hear," I said with a chuckle. "He really is amazing. I'm stunned that no one tried to steal him when you were in town, to be honest."

"No one could, even if they wanted to. He won't let most people near him. I'm surprised he hasn't tried to bite your arm off, if I'm being honest."

I jerked my hand back, and Aithan snickered.

"I'm joking," he said. "Sort of. Come, let's mount up. It's only about a ten-minute ride to the cabin, if we move quickly."

Tyrannus' gait was smooth and quick. It wasn't a trot or a

canter—more like a very fast walk that made me feel like I was riding a fast-moving conveyor belt.

The scenery passed by as the first flakes of fluffy snow began to fall, coating the surrounding lands in a soft, white blanket.

As we advanced, the trees began to grow taller, thicker, and the road narrowed until it was all but impassable...as though the woods were pulling us into a well-laid trap.

"I can see why you move around on horseback," I said, holding on loosely to Aithan's waist. "The snow in the forest is so deep, I'm not sure if I could trudge through it without dying of exhaustion."

"Horses are handy," he replied. "But Grells are the ones who are best suited for this territory—they generally have the easiest time on the varied terrain. And Waergs, of course. Anyone sure-footed, really. You'll see what I mean as we approach the cliffs."

Sure enough, just a few minutes later, a massive wall of stone and ice appeared before us in the distance, just visible through the blustery snow. Jagged and sheer, it looked like the sort of thing only the most coordinated mountain goat could climb.

Strange, glowing red lines criss-crossed its surface like pulsing marble veins, and above the cliff's upper edge, the mountain beyond kept growing until it disappeared into the gray skies above.

"Caffall has been staying up on the mountain?" I asked.

"No. They say he dwells inside the Slash."

"The Slash?"

"A large cave—shaped like a long stab wound—midway up the cliff. It's broad and deep, and they say it's been occupied by dragons since the beginning of time."

"So I'm supposed to climb halfway up that wall in order to find my way to him?"

"Unless you have a better way to get there, yeah."

I ground my jaw and stared at the imposing cliff. "I have a

better way," I said. "If I can picture it in my mind's eye, I can get there without risking my neck."

"Trust me—what you'll find inside is far more likely to kill you than the fall."

"Thanks for the vote of confidence."

WE ARRIVED at Aithan's cabin after a few minutes. It looked as I'd expected—a house made entirely of large, rough-hewn logs, with smoke billowing from a chunky brick chimney. A small paddock and stable for Tyrannus sat to one side of the house, and a shaggy donkey stood waiting for his friend's return.

A large, furry black dog the size of a small bear came bounding out to greet us upon our arrival, his tongue hanging out. As we dismounted, he leapt at Aithan, his front paws on the Ranger's shoulders, licking his face as if he hadn't seen him in years.

"Meet Fafnir," Aithan said. "The most useless guard dog of all time."

"He's amazing," I replied, crouching down to scratch Fafnir's chest, which was emblazoned with a white star.

Somehow, any fear I had of spending the night in a relative stranger's house dissipated with the knowledge that he had such an excellent dog for a companion.

As I stared at the house, I turned around to see that Aithan was attaching something to Fafnir's tail. It looked at first glance like a large fan made of soft straw.

"What are you doing?" I asked as the dog went bounding off in the direction we'd come from, the strange device dragging in the fresh snow behind him.

"Covering up our tracks," Aithan said. "After your little stunt in the pub, I expect word will get out that there's a Shadow about. Which means Sassers will be keeping their eyes out for you. The

Sweeper will conceal our tracks, and it's coated in Ursal musk, which ensures that Waergs will stay far away from us for now."

"Clever trick. Smart dog, too."

"Yeah, he's good for something, at least," my host laughed.

When Aithan had removed Tyrannus' tack and let him into the paddock to nuzzle at his donkey friend's muzzle, we headed inside, where embers were glowing in a large, open stone fireplace that opened out both into the living room and the kitchen.

As I watched, Aithan headed through the kitchen to what looked like a silver refrigerator and opened it, pulling out a plate of cheese and meat.

"I didn't expect to see a fridge," I admitted. "I forget there's electricity in the Otherwhere sometimes."

"Not just electricity," he replied, waving a hand in the air above the kitchen table.

A large, translucent screen appeared in front of us, displaying a 3-dimensional topographical map.

"That's the terrain around here," Aithan said, pointing to a tree-coated spot near the base of a mountain. "You are here."

Awestruck by the technology, I studied our surroundings. Dense forest ran along the base of the mountain, though that was no surprise. The cliff extended for miles in both directions, wrapping itself around the mountain like a protective wall.

At its center was a horizontal gash that looked a little like a menacing eye.

"The Slash," Aithan said, confirming the theory that was already forming in my mind. "We think that's where Caffall is. It was inhabited until recently by a Flame-Drake who left the minute the golden dragon showed up, rather than engage with such an impressive foe."

"Are there any houses or towns between here and the cliff?" I asked. "Anything I should know about?"

"There's a house near the base of the cliff…here," Aithan said, pointing to a spot to the northwest of our current location. "It was deserted for years, but recently seems to have been taken over by an old man—the sort who likes to dwell in the mountains, away from civilization. I first spotted him several days ago, on one of our rides. He looked harmless enough, so I gave him space."

"He wasn't a Ranger?"

"No...he looked old and decrepit. I was surprised he was this far away from civilization, truth be told. I assume he's here to escape society—a true mountain man. Word in town has it that he saw the inside of the Slash once, many years ago. They say he's the only one who's ever seen it."

"I see. No one else?"

"No."

"Okay, then," I said, taking a piece of cheese and popping it into my mouth. "I'm going to go see the old man."

"You're serious? Why would you do that?"

"He's the only one who's seen the cave up there. I need detail. A description. I need to be able to picture it vividly."

"Vega, I don't know him. He could be mad, for all I know. This could be extremely dangerous."

"I'll take my chances," I shrugged, looking around. "Do you have a big coat? A scarf? Anything I can wear under my cloak?"

"You're seriously planning to hike out to his cabin?"

"Of course. Unless you have a better idea."

Aithan let out a frustrated sigh. "Tyrannus and I will bring you. Come on, then."

THE OLD MAN

WE RODE for what felt like half an hour. The snow was falling heavily now, and Fafnir was bounding along beside us happily, seemingly oblivious to the bitter wind that burned my cheeks even as I tried to shield myself behind Aithan's broad shoulders.

"I should stay with you when we reach the house," the Ranger told me, shouting to be heard over the wind. "It would only be right."

"No," I replied, squinting into the distance and trying to make out the lines of the trees through the wall of falling snow. "I'd prefer that you didn't. I need information, and he's less likely to give it if he knows there's a man with deadly weapons standing around outside."

"Vega, like I said, he could be less than sane. He might try to hurt you."

"A lot of people have tried to hurt me over the past couple of months," I replied with a cynical chuckle. "I'm still alive. So thank you, but it's all right."

"Fine. But I'll be in the woods, watching. Final offer."

"Fair enough. Just do me one favor."

"What's that?"

"If you see me summon a door, stay back. Stay hidden. And if I walk through it, just go home."

"Vega..."

"Just promise me."

"Fine. I promise."

A few minutes later, I spotted a small clearing ahead. It sat some distance from the base of the cliff, which looked even more imposing than I'd imagined, now that I could see it in all its glory.

The red veins I'd noticed earlier pulsed even brighter now, criss-crossing the stone and ice as if they were some sort of invasive species looking to take over the entire cliff face.

At my request, Aithan stopped before the edge of the woods, quietly calling Fafnir to his side.

"Thank you," I said. "I may make my way back to your house later, if that's okay."

"May? You're not sure?"

"It's entirely possible that I won't," I shrugged. "My only goal right now is to find Caffall. If I manage to do that in the next hour or so, I see no reason that we'll see each other again tonight."

"You're quite mad. Has anyone ever told you that?"

"Not in so many words. But I'm beginning to think I should wear it as a badge of honor," I laughed. "You do have to be a little loopy to be a Seeker. And I'm seeking the ultimate treasure right now."

"Yeah, well, you wouldn't think he'd be all that hard to find. He's pretty big, in case you hadn't noticed."

"I'm well aware. And from what I hear, he's likely to torment La Baie's residents again this evening. If possible, I'd like to get to him before he burns any more houses to the ground."

"Suit yourself, lunatic."

I dismounted, smiled up at Aithan, and said, "Look after yourself, okay?"

"Of course."

"And whatever you might see happening in the next little while—try to resist the urge to come barging into the old man's cabin to save the day."

"Barging in to save the day is my specialty. I'm a Ranger. It's what I do."

"I don't need saving. Bye for now, Aithan."

"Bye, Vega Sloane."

I turned away with a final pat to Fafnir's head and proceeded to trek through the snow toward the cabin that was just barely visible through the sea of tumbling flakes.

As I approached, I could see smoke rising from the chimney, and in the window, the flicker of what looked like a lantern.

The place looked like Santa Claus' house. It was all but beckoning me over for a visit.

I could only hope its owner was as friendly as Santa himself.

When I'd finally made it, I knocked on the door and stomped my snow-covered boots on the small wooden porch, waiting.

After a few seconds, the door creaked open to reveal a man in a long brown tunic, his shoulders hunched forward with age. His beard was white and long, his eyes cloudy as he tried to narrow them into focus.

"Who are you?" he asked in a gruff tone.

"Someone who's interested in the golden dragon who's been hanging out in the cliff above you," I said. "I'm assuming you're not too happy he's there."

The man pulled his eyes skyward and shook his head. "No, none too happy. But he hasn't given me any trouble, at least not yet. His tastes are more…urban."

"Well, I'm hoping to persuade him to leave this part of the Otherwhere, with your help," I said. "May I come in?"

The man eyed me as if he was trying to decide whether to let me cross the threshold or slice me in half, then grudgingly backed away and gestured for me to enter.

The inside of the small cabin was rustic, to put it mildly. Scattered here and there was a patchwork of ancient, rickety-looking furniture that looked on the verge of collapse. A set of antlers from some poor animal that looked like it had been scalped was hanging on the wall above the fireplace. Dirty dishes lay on every surface, ratty blankets lying across every piece of uncomfortable-looking furniture.

"They say you're the only person around here who knows the cavern where the dragon's been staying," I said, turning to look at the man. "You've climbed the cliff? You've seen the Slash?"

He nodded. "I have been up there, yes. Many moons ago."

"Can you describe it for me?"

Instead of a reply, the man turned and walked toward the kitchen, where a kettle had just started whistling. I was impressed, not to mention surprised, that he was able to hear the high-pitched squeal even before my own ears picked it up.

"I will consider describing it for you on one condition," my reluctant host said as he turned the heat down on his stove and pulled the kettle off the burner.

"What condition is that?" I asked, stepping into the kitchen.

He turned my way and locked his eyes on mine. For a second their cloudiness seemed to clear away, and they turned dark brown, almost black. "Tell me, what will you do when you get to the cavern?"

"I can't tell you that," I said. "Partly because I don't know the answer yet."

"Why would a girl like you want to be going anywhere near a beast like the golden dragon? It doesn't make any sense. He is a killer. A torcher of homes. He is a destructive force, and nothing more."

I chewed on my cheek for a moment, contemplating how much I could tell him without risking giving myself entirely away. "That dragon is part of someone I care about," I said.

"Ah. The would-be king, you mean."

His misted eyes were locked on mine, and I felt imprisoned, as if I had no choice but to answer.

"You...you know about the prophecy?"

"Of course I do," the man said. "I've lived in the Otherwhere for many, many years. I know of a certain young man's exile, and the Usurper Queen's takeover of the throne that rightfully belongs to someone else...or so they say. Well, good luck to you, girl. I hope everything goes as you'd like it to."

"Thank you," I said, my tone impatient. "Now, this condition of yours...?"

The man chuckled. "Chomping at the bit, are ya?"

I glared at him. I was in no mood for games.

"Fine," he said. "I only want you to retrieve something from La Baie for me. A mere trinket—an object that once belonged to my family. I'm too old and tired to venture there on my own, but something tells me you could find your way there quickly, with help from your horse-owning friend. Or perhaps another way."

"I see." So, he knew about Aithan. He may even have known about my ability to summon doors.

Still, I was beginning to think he was a few cards short of a deck. A trinket? What could this man—with his rickety furnishings and freezing-cold cabin—possibly want with a trinket?

"And where do I find this item of yours?" I asked.

"That's for you to tell me. You, and the dragon."

I was growing angry by now. The man was toying with me, surely. He talked in riddles—and not even interesting ones.

"I don't have time for games," I told him. "I need you to tell me what to do. Give me a hint. *Something.* Otherwise, our deal is off. I can get to the dragon on my own, if I have to."

"Fine, fine." The hunched man seemed to straighten a little as he said, "Begin by returning to La Baie tonight. But be wary. The dragon will show his face after dark, and when he does, he will wreak havoc. But follow his trail, and you will find what you're looking for. Bring the item to me when you have it, and I will instruct you further."

"You're not even telling me what it is I'm looking for!" I snapped. "How do I know you're not just some whacko who lives in a shack and is stealing something valuable from someone unfortunate?"

"I may well be. But something tells me you're willing to take that chance. You have a desire to commune with the dragon, and I have a desire to possess the trinket. It's quite a simple deal, really."

Too annoyed to say anything more, I strode toward the door, turning only when I'd opened it. "Fine. I'll be back once I've found whatever mystery item I'm looking for," I told the nameless man. "When I return, you'd better be here."

"Don't worry. I wouldn't dream of leaving."

Outside, I moved into the clearing, scanning the woods for Aithan. When I'd spotted him tucked some distance into the forest with Fafnir by his side, I gave him a subtle nod before closing my eyes and calling up a door to La Baie.

Go home, Ranger, I thought. *And never come back to this place.*

AN UNEXPECTED GUEST

I CAME through the door I'd summoned in a dark, narrow alley behind the Grell and Grimestone pub, where the familiar scent of frying fish immediately hit me square in the face.

Pulling my cloak around me, my hood over my head, I made my way in through the pub's back entrance and wandered through the kitchen to a series of glances by employees who sniffed the air briefly before refocusing on their tasks.

When I'd made my way out of the kitchen, I headed straight for the bar, where the same bartender I'd met earlier was still working.

"You again," he grumbled when I sat down. "I don't want any trouble, Miss. I hope your Ranger friend isn't planning on showing up."

"Not as far as I know," I assured him. "Listen, do you know what time it is?"

He glanced toward the window, assessed the daylight for a moment, then turned back to me. "I'd say it's nearing dusk. Five or so."

"Good. Thanks. Um, what time does the golden dragon usually show up?"

The bartender, who was in the process of cleaning a glass, nearly dropped it.

"Now, why on earth would you want to know a thing like that?" he asked.

"Curiosity," I said with what I hoped looked like an innocent shrug.

"If we're all damned lucky, he won't show up at all. That creature is a menace, and it's only a matter of days before he destroys this street and every business on it. You mark my words."

Remembering what Solara had advised, I pulled my hood away from my face, lowered my chin, and gave the man my most charming smile.

I could only hope he wouldn't sense how forced it was.

"Please tell me," I simpered. "I'm just...so curious to see him."

The man set the glass down and leaned forward, his elbows on the bar. A slow, twisted grin slipped over his chapped lips, and I had to struggle not to recoil in revulsion.

"Well now, Sweetheart, since you asked so nicely, he usually comes around six or seven. He seems to like the place just as night's properly falling. Maybe because he can see all the lights on in the windows. He probably thinks this town's full of delicious snacks." The bartender winked. "But mind that you stay out of his way. It would be a shame to see a pretty face like yours burned to a crisp."

I shuddered. How were some men so adept at issuing compliments that instantly made my skin crawl?

"Thank you. I definitely will. I promise."

The bartender headed off to deal with a grumpy-looking Grell at the far end of the bar, and I pulled my hood back up around my face, a scowl setting itself on my features.

This town seemed to be sorely lacking in women, and I missed the friendly, supportive Sisterhood of Aradia. I found myself wishing for Solara's reassuring presence. There was a confidence in her that I'd never encountered in any woman—not even my own very strong mother or my Nana, two of the of the most staunchly self-assured people I'd ever met.

I found myself wishing for Niala's presence, too. She was young like me, but had an otherworldly calm about her that had always reminded me of Callum. She seldom panicked or lost her cool. She was the perfect sort of Healer—a rock-solid person who could soothe the nerves of any patient, even one whose chances of survival were slim to none.

But of course, Niala was with Callum at the Academy's infirmary, along with Rourke and Merriwether.

Still...I found myself picturing her next to me, keeping me from tensing under the hungry gaze of so many strange males.

"I believe you summoned me, Miss Sloane."

The voice came from behind me, smooth and even, a smile coloring its edges.

I spun around in my seat to see Niala standing in front of me, dressed in a cloak similar to mine.

Only hers was a rich hunter green.

Rourke's ferret head was poking out from between the folds of the garment, his eyes staring intently at me.

"I didn't summon you!" I assured her. "Or did I? Maybe I did, by accident." I rose to my feet and hugged her tight. "But I'm so happy you're here."

"Me, too. I'm happy to see you in one piece. You look...strong."

I smiled, staring into her cat-like eyes before inviting her to take a seat next to me.

"I'm sorry," I said. "It was selfish of me to call you here. I was just feeling so alone. But you should go back, shouldn't you? Callum is..."

"Callum is fine," she said, clasping her hands on top of the bar. "You have nothing to worry about."

"He's fine?" I asked. "Really?"

"Really. There's been no change since you left. He's still

unconscious, but perfectly restful. He's probably having some pleasant dreams right about now—I administered a few drops of a solution designed to bring his fondest memories to the forefront of his mind."

"That's good to know," I told her. "Because I haven't managed to talk to Caffall yet." I laughed. "That sounds so stupid. Like I'm waiting for a business meeting with the dragon so I can renegotiate his mortgage or something."

"I'm sure you'll find a way." Niala looked around the pub, shifting her gaze quickly back to me. "Do I dare ask where Lachlan is?"

For a second, I buried my face in my hands and let out another bitter laugh, followed by a moan. "He was injured while he was protecting me. The Witches of Aradia have him. It seems I leave a trail of wounded male bodies wherever I go, doesn't it?"

"The Witches?" Niala said with a slightly goofy grin. "You really met Lady Solara's Coven? I'm envious."

"Lady Solara," I repeated. "She didn't call herself that, but I suppose it makes sense. She has a regal sort of quality to her."

"She's supposed to be incredible," Niala said. "Tell me, what are the Witches like?"

"You'd like them. They remind me of you. And they're really into healing. They have some impressive skills."

"So I've heard. Maybe after all this is over—after you've figured out the dragon situation—you could introduce me to them?"

"I'd love to. They were impressed with the healing salve you gave me, actually. They'd be only too happy to meet you, too." I shot a sideways glance over to the bartender, who was several feet away and occupied with a couple of unruly Grells, then added, "Listen—would you come for a walk with me?"

"Of course. I'm here, aren't I? It's not like I have anything better to do."

We left the pub and wandered down the street. The sky was

darkening with a layer of low, thick cloud cover, and instantly, a chill set into my flesh that didn't entirely seem to come from the wintery conditions.

"They say the dragon's been terrorizing this town each evening," I said as we strolled. "Burning down houses for no apparent reason. I need to watch his movements tonight."

"You're waiting for him to show up and torch the place? Why?"

"Because," I chewed my lip for a second, trying to work out how to tell her about the strange old man's request. "I'm supposed to follow his trail."

"As usual, I'm baffled," Niala said. "But you always seem to know what you're doing, so I'll go alone with it, Vega."

"Thanks. I should warn you, though—it could get dangerous. By that, I mean it'll *definitely* get dangerous."

"I'm hanging about with Vega Sloane, and danger is stalking us. Surprise, surprise."

I let out a chuckle. "I'm a mess, aren't I? It's a wonder anyone ever comes near me."

"Some people are drawn to danger. It's no surprise that men like Callum or Lachlan would find you alluring. You're the living embodiment of excitement."

"That's ridiculous," I told her. "I'm the most boring person in the world."

"Lachlan doesn't seem to think so."

"So you know about him, then," I said, kicking at a loose stone that went rolling along the cobbled street ahead of us.

"I know he feels something for you, yes. It doesn't take a clairvoyant to see that."

"Well, I wish he'd stop...*feeling* things. It's not good for him, or me, or Liv, or anyone."

"If we could turn our feelings off and on, life would be simple, wouldn't it?" Niala asked as Rourke leapt out of her cloak onto the ground.

"What's up with him?" I asked, glad for the excuse to change the subject.

He pushed himself up onto his hind legs, his tiny front paws hovering in front of his chest, and looked up at the sky.

Niala grabbed my arm and followed Rourke's gaze.

"What is it?" I asked. "Does he see something?"

"More like feels something," she replied slowly. "He says…the dragon is coming."

DRAGON FIRE

THE SKY BEGAN to glow a reddish-orange, as if a distant forest fire was threatening an approach. But the glow intensified quickly, flame seemingly soaring on the clouds above us in a hurricane-force wind.

Nearby, people shouted. Women cried out for their children to come inside their houses. Men bellowed that it was happening again—that the town was doomed, that they were being punished for some nameless sin.

And all I could think about was the prophecy. The one that stated the heir of the Otherwhere would turn the land to ash... unless he found his mysterious "Treasure."

Caffall was as much the heir to the throne as Callum was. He was single-handedly turning the prophecy into truth, beginning in the Northwest. It was only a matter of time before he'd work his way to the other regions of this world. He would burn the towns and fields of Anara. He would ravage what was left of Kaer Uther. He would scorch the forests and mountains until there was nothing left.

Unless I found a way to stop him.

As Niala and I stood frozen, the massive, metallic-gold belly of the dragon glided over us like the bottom of a ship. A cry—a piercing, banshee-like wail that rattled the windows of the houses around us—rang through the darkness in a harsh warning.

"What are you doing, Caffall?" I mouthed. "And why?"

"We'd better move if we're to follow his trail," Niala warned me.

"Right, of course."

Rourke shifted into his panther form and together, we began to jog along the street in the direction Caffall had flown.

Throngs of townsfolk, meanwhile, were fleeing in the opposite direction. Some were in their wolf forms, others sprinting along on hybrid Grell legs. Occasionally, someone would yell, "What are you doing? Go back! He'll kill you!" but we ignored them and raced after our target.

It was at the far end of town that Caffall paused in mid-flight, setting his sights on a row of houses. We arrived just in time to see him begin his onslaught, a stream of flame shooting from his mouth, taking down house after house, even as some of the stragglers fled for their lives.

We watched in horror as the wooden abodes burned and the dragon, apparently sated, turned and flew back toward the cliffs where he'd come from.

"I don't understand!" I shouted, tears streaming down my face. It was shocking—horrifying—to see a part of Callum being so utterly destructive and cruel. "Why would he do this?"

"Maybe he's lost," Niala said as Rourke stalked ahead of us toward the still raging trail of flame. "He's confused. He has no purpose without Callum, just as Callum has no purpose without him. So he's feeding off his basest instincts."

"I need to find a way to break through to him. It's not right that he's doing this to these poor people."

We kept walking until the flames' heat met our bodies,

warning us to stay back. I scanned the area, wondering where to start my search for the "trinket" the old man had requested.

I was just surveying the area when a familiar silhouette appeared from out of the darkness. A young man astride a large dappled horse.

Rourke tightened, raising his back like a house cat threatening a dog.

"It's all right," I assured him. "That's Aithan."

Niala immediately smiled. "No way!" she said, running toward the rider, who leapt off his horse and gave her a hug.

"You know each other?" I asked as I approached, wiping the last of the tears from my face.

"We do. The Rangers come and go from the Academy," Niala said as Aithan held a hand out for Rourke to sniff. "I've treated this one more than once in the infirmary."

I couldn't help but smile to look at her. I'd never seen Niala looking quite so happy to see anyone, and couldn't help wondering if there was more to their story than she was letting on.

"I see," I said, resisting a wink and a nudge.

"I was worried when you didn't come back," Aithan said. "I saw the dragon flying overhead, so I made my way here. What the hell are you two doing so close to the fire?"

I explained as quickly as I could why I needed to trace Caffall's route. "I'm not entirely sure what I'm looking for," I confessed. "Just that it's important."

"I'm not sure you should trust the old man," Aithan said. "He's a strange one. Comes and goes. Never seems to need food. Disappears like he was never there. He may simply be toying with you—or trying to get you murdered."

"I don't care, as long as he holds up his end of the deal," I said. "He's the only hope I have right now."

"Fair enough. Let's get looking then, shall we? You say we're supposed to follow the trail?"

"Yeah. Though it's not much of one. Just a fiery mess, really."

I nodded toward the house next to me, which had all but collapsed on itself, the wood beams snapped like brittle bones.

"Vega," Niala said, pointing. "Look—in one of the beams—there's an opening."

I glanced over to see that she was right. There was a rectangular recess in one of the shattered hunks of wood.

And inside, something—an object of some sort—was tucked tight.

I walked over to get a closer look, only to see something tarnished and silver that looked like a short walking stick. At one end was an ornament shaped like a dragon in flight.

"Is it a cane?" I asked.

"Too short to be a cane," said Aithan. "Looks like a scepter."

"A scepter? Like the kind of thing a king or queen holds onto?"

"Yes, that kind of thing."

"What's it doing here?" I asked. But even as the words formed on my tongue, a feeling of nausea began to churn inside me. "Unless..." I added.

"Unless what?"

I shook my head. "Nothing. Let's grab it."

"It'll be scorching hot," Niala warned.

But I was already stepping into the sea of embers. I wasn't sure if I'd gone numb or if there was some sort of magic at play. But I didn't feel my boots melting under my soles, nor was I even breaking into a sweat. The searing heat had died down to nothing, despite the flames that still surrounded me.

And when I reached for the scepter, it was cool to the touch.

"Got it," I said with a smile, turning to the other two. "Let's go to your place, Aithan."

"Fine, but Tyr can't take all three of us. He's strong, but that's pushing it."

"I'll open a Breach. I've already used my magic; at this point, it's not like it'll give me away any more than it already has."

Niala and Aithan agreed, and I called up a door to Aithan's isolated abode. It was broad as a barn door, and tall enough for Tyrannus to walk through, though he was hesitant at first.

When Aithan had put him into the stable for the night and we'd gone inside, I told the other two I was leaving first thing in the morning.

"I have no choice," I shot out when they protested. "I can't bear to wait any longer. The more time that passes, the greater the risk to La Baie, not to mention Callum. I need to do what I can to end this madness."

"Anything we can help with?" Aithan asked as he handed me a cup of hot cocoa.

"Sure. You can search for my body…if things go badly tomorrow."

HOPE

"Come on, now. Why would things go badly?" Niala asked. "I thought you were just handing the scepter over to some old mountain man."

I sucked on my cheeks to stop myself from saying anything more.

Maybe the old man was exactly who he claimed to be. A half-blind hermit who chose to isolate himself from the world, and whose family had once owned a pretty scepter.

Or maybe he was something else entirely.

"You're right," I said. "It's just a simple transaction. I'll be fine."

"You know I've got your back, whatever happens," Niala said. "All I want is your happiness, and for you to find a way to bring Callum back from the brink."

"Thanks. I know you do."

After a moment, Aithan asked, "What sort of life do you think would make you happy, Vega?"

I took a sip of my cocoa and let out a long breath. "That's a big question," I replied. "But a good one. You know, I've never managed to picture a future for myself in my own world. Adulthood. A career. Marriage. It's like I always assumed I'd end up like my Nana, living alone in a house on a cliff somewhere, away from prying eyes or judgmental glares. But maybe it's just that I somehow knew I would end up here, in the Otherwhere. Even when I was little, I pictured myself in another place and time. I used to imagine unicorns and fairies, and all sorts of creatures that don't exist in my world. Maybe it's because I was meant to be here all along."

"Maybe," Niala said, "this is what you were meant to do since the day you were born. If you save Callum's life—if you save Caffall from whatever madness has overtaken him—you will be a true heroine in this world. A legend. You don't know what a momentous achievement it would be, Vega."

"I *do* know," I told her, my eyes going misty with tears. "Because I love Callum. I know how much others love him, too. And if all the Otherwhere knew him like we do, they would want him on that throne even more badly than they already do. They would want him to lead them. They would rally behind him."

"And behind you, if you were to share the throne with him."

"Callum may get sick of me," I said. "There's no guarantee that he'll want to stay with me, let alone want to share a throne with me."

"You've clearly never watched him when he's looking at you," Niala laughed. "I've never seen a man so madly in love. Don't forget—he's not some fickle boy. He's lived a long life and never once fallen for anyone. He was waiting until he *knew*."

I smiled. It was true. After over a century of life, Callum had chosen me, and me alone, to be his partner—though our partnership had its obvious limitations. The fact that we lived in two different worlds wasn't exactly helpful.

"I shouldn't even let myself daydream about it," I said, laying my mug down on a wooden stool by the fireplace and pushing myself to my feet. "It's not like I can just up and move here. There's Will to think about. And Liv." I stretched, yawned, and turned to Aithan. "I'm sorry to break up our little party, but is there somewhere I could sleep until dawn?" I asked.

"Yes, of course. Back room, to the right. There's a bathroom across the way with everything you'll need."

"Thank you," I said. "You two enjoy yourselves. I'll be gone by the time you wake up, and I'm not sure when I'll see you again."

"I'll bring Niala back to the Academy if it comes down to it," Aithan assured me. "But I really wish you'd let us come with you in the morning."

"I know. I just think I need to do this alone."

"All right," Niala said, throwing a shy look Aithan's way. "I think I'm going to stay up for a little. It will be nice to catch up."

"Okay then. Good night." As I walked away, I smiled and muttered, "Something tells me you're going to be doing more than catching up, my friend."

REVELATIONS

The night was too long and too short at once.

Clutching the scepter tight in my hand, I tossed and turned, waiting for the sun to rise, yet fearful of what would happen when it did.

If the old man fulfilled his part of our bargain...and *if* I then managed to find Caffall, I was still skeptical as to whether this insane plan of mine would work. I'd watched the golden dragon turn part of La Baie into a bonfire. He was a destruction machine. A monster.

A feeling of unease began to grow inside me as the night progressed. Much as it had been fun to relax and enjoy Niala's and Aithan's company, the darkness and quiet of the night seemed to shroud me in anxiety. I found myself asking what could possibly happen in the morning, other than that I'd hand over the scepter to a dubious character and then get my butt handed to me by a very angry dragon?

Still, my gut told me there was a reason I'd retrieved that scepter. There was a reason I'd met the old man. And Aithan.

And there was a reason I'd ended up here in the wilds of the Northwest.

I only wished I felt better about my chances of success.

When the first glow of dawn finally began to creep through my window, I forced myself to get up and dress once again in the black clothing Solara had given me. I splashed cold water on my face, looked at myself in the bathroom's mirror, and assured myself that I was going to succeed.

Judging by my expression, though, the promise wasn't remotely convincing.

Tiptoeing through Aithan's cabin, I made my way outside, the scepter in hand, only to be greeted by the sting of bitterly cold wind. When I was standing some distance from the house, I called up a Breach to the edge of the clearing where the old man's cabin stood.

A few seconds later, I found myself staring at the small, unassuming shack near the base of the cliff. I was trembling not so much from cold as something else, something deep inside myself that feared the possibly catastrophic repercussions of what I was about to do.

By now, I knew without a shadow of a doubt that the scepter in my hand—the "trinket," as the man called it—was no mere family heirloom. It was precious beyond imagining, and even without being told its true origins, I knew at least some of its value.

I also knew that handing it to him would be a betrayal of all that I stood for.

But it was also the only hope I had of getting Callum back.

With a deep breath, I stepped forward, only to see the cabin's door opening inward.

"Ah," the man said, moving into the doorway and straightening up from his usual hunched position, his eyes locking on mine. "I see you've brought the trinket."

"I have," I said, hesitant to move any closer. "But before I give it to you, I need you to tell me about the cavern known as the Slash."

"Certainly," the man replied. "The entrance," he said, admiring the scepter in my hand, his gaze slipping over the ornate dragon at its end, "is a hundred or so feet long, twenty or so feet high. Its interior glows an arctic, icy blue, and its floor is littered with the bones of bears, deer, and other forest-dwelling creatures… including Waergs. There is a broad, white hearth inside, its mantel decorated with still more bones." He pulled his eyes to mine. "Of course, its most recognizable feature is the pile of human skulls that sits just outside the mouth of the cave."

"Human skulls?" I asked. "Really?"

"Really. Now, do you have enough to picture it?"

"I…I think so," I said, the image forming in my mind.

Yes, I could feel it now. His description had given me enough to summon a Breach. To reach the cavern in seconds, and to find my way to the golden dragon who might char-broil me the instant he set eyes on me.

"Good. Then I believe it's time you gave me the scepter, isn't it?"

I stepped toward him and reached my hand out, but pulled back at the last second.

"Wait," I said.

I could feel his impatience as he ground his jaw and growled, "What is it now?"

"I want you to show me who you really are."

The man smiled what almost looked like a grin of relief as he altered in front of me.

The deepest of the lines faded from his face. His hair thickened and darkened, his beard disappeared. He was suddenly handsome, his cheekbones high and elegant, and, most striking of all, he was dressed entirely in a white, tailored three-piece suit.

His posture changed too, and he straightened up to reveal a tall, slim frame. He didn't even remotely resemble the old man I'd encountered—the man who had asked me to retrieve his family heirloom.

"You don't look altogether surprised," he told me as I stepped backward, examining him. "Though you don't look pleased, either, to see me as I truly am."

"You're a wizard," I said.

"I am. But of course, you're familiar with my kind because of that grandfather of yours." The man let out a sigh and once again stroked his gaze over the scepter that I still held tightly. "He's none too happy with me at the moment."

As I stared at him, the full gravity of what I'd done assaulted me.

I'd made a deal with the devil.

"You're Marauth," I choked.

"I am. And I believe *that* is mine."

He held out his hand, and I hesitated for only a second before handing the scepter over.

He held it up with a grim smile, examining it, and as he did so, its stains seemed to fade away. Its silver brightened and even glowed in the pale sunlight breaking through the clouds above. "You have given me a gift, Seeker. You don't know what it means to me." Running a hand through his thick head of hair, he added, "The moment you touched the scepter you knew what it was, didn't you? You knew what you were sacrificing."

"A Seeker knows when she comes upon a Relic of Power," I replied. "But I didn't know who you were. Not exactly. I only suspected."

"You gave it willingly, even after you learned who and what I am," Marauth said. "There is no taking it back, not now." With a deep, satisfied laugh, he added, "Come in out of the cold, won't you?"

"No. I don't think I will," I replied, pulling my eyes to the imposing cliff beyond his cabin. "I have a dragon to see."

With that, Marauth's lips twisted into a cruel smile. "You are an impressive, if foolish, girl, aren't you?"

"You think he'll kill me," I said. "You think Caffall will burn me alive, just for fun."

"Perhaps," he shrugged. "Perhaps not. Let's just say you'll find him changed since the last time you saw him. To be honest, I couldn't care less if you end up dead in the next few minutes, Vega."

"You're a sick man," I snarled.

"Yes. I'm a sick man, with a very lovely, very important Relic that a Seeker has willingly handed me," he replied. "If you only knew the history of this exquisite piece..." He was still eyeing the scepter, as though mesmerized by its contours. "If you only knew to whom it once belonged..."

"I don't care about any of that," I said with a scowl. "I'm leaving you now. You can do whatever the hell you want with your *trinket*." I was tempted to go further, but I wasn't sure I wanted my last words to be "Shove the scepter where the sun doesn't shine, Wizard."

"Good, good...fine..." Marauth replied, his voice distant, his eyes still locked on the Relic of Power as if I no longer existed.

I left him in the doorway of his odd little cabin, and, terrified of the fate that awaited me, made my way toward the base of the cliff.

INTO THE DRAGON'S DEN

THE DOOR I summoned to take me to the Slash was carved with the long, serpentine shape of a dragon. On his head was a crown of golden spikes, much like the one I'd seen the last time I'd set eyes on Caffall.

Nervous, I pulled the dragon key off its silver chain around my neck and unlocked the door, pulling it open slowly, half expecting a bolt of flame to shoot through and end my life on the spot.

But I stepped through into a world of bluish shadows, my eyes landing immediately on the white hearth Marauth had described, a few feet from where I stood. What looked like two human femurs were sitting, crossed, on its mantel.

"Well, *that's* a bad sign," I muttered.

I turned to see that the cavern was massive, its floor an uneven layer of glacial terrain. And as I took my first step toward its gaping wound of an entrance, two bright, massive eyes blinked at me from the shadows.

"Caffall," I breathed inadvertently, my breath misting in front of my face.

The dragon pulled his head up and huffed out a smoky warning, his mouth opening to reveal a set of glistening teeth, each as tall as me.

"Caffall," I said again, holding a hand out as I moved toward him. "That is your name, isn't it? You remember me, don't you?"

I took another tentative step, but stopped when a deep rumble vibrated its way through my mind, like a voice reaching out to me.

Only it wasn't human.

Not even close.

Three words came to me:

Vega...the Seeker.

"Yes," I said, smiling through my anxiety, hoping to keep him calm. "It's me."

You wish to help me—and Lord Drake.

"I do," I told him. "Callum needs us both. You and I—we need to save him."

The dragon pulled his head up, shaking it as if trying to free himself from a snare, another low, terrifying growl churning in his throat.

He broke an ancient law. He said my name.

"He did it to protect the Otherwhere," I said, taking another unsteady step toward him. "He did it so I could take the Lyre of Adair to Merriwether. But he wasn't trying to hurt you."

*Hurt me? He didn't **hurt** me. He helped me.*

"What do you mean?"

He gave me what I've always desired. My Treasure...my freedom.

"Treasure," I said. "Like in the prophecy. This is what you've always wanted?"

I've always wanted to be free, yes. But I did not wish to be severed from Lord Drake. I do not wish him harm. I have been looking for the means to return to him. Looking, every night, in that wretched place...

I had no idea what he meant. But I wasn't about to question a dragon's sanity.

At least, not to his face.

"Tell me what I can do to help," I said, moving toward him, my hand extended.

As if in warning, Caffall pulled his head back, shooting out a dart of flame that struck the ice directly in front of my feet. I leapt back, shrieking, and the dragon twisted around and flew out of the cave.

I dashed after him, helpless to stop him.

"What is it?" I shouted. "What happened? Did I do something wrong?"

I watched him fly off over the trees, fully expecting him to disappear, never to return. But after a few seconds, he banked hard to the right and circled back toward the Slash, his voice echoing through my mind.

You found it last night. You found the means to reunite us.

He soared toward the cavern's opening then stopped, flapping his massive wings to hover fifty feet or so from the cave's entrance.

"The means?" I asked. "What means?"

You gave it to the man. You gave away the solution.

"You know him?" I asked. "You know the man in the cabin?"

I know he is not a friend. I know he wishes me ill. He does not want Lord Drake to wake up.

There was hatred in the dragon's tone.

You should not have given it to him. You have destroyed our one chance.

"I don't get it—how do you even know what I found?"

I've been searching for the object since my arrival in Dragonhelm. I knew Marauth was searching for it...I knew his intentions. Tell me, do you know why he wanted the scepter?

"It's a Relic of Power," I said. "It will make him stronger."

It is much more than that, Vega Sloane. You see, Marauth believes that with it, he can prevent the true king from waking, or from taking the throne. The wizard's one and only goal is to keep the scepter out of the hands of those who can use it to save Lord Drake's life.

"Are you seriously saying the scepter could have helped Callum?" I asked, my voice shaking. "But how?"

Caffall simply replied, *If you wish to understand, then you must find a way to take the Relic of Power back from the wizard.*

"I can't just take it back! I gave it to him in exchange for information. I can't just snatch a Relic of Power back from someone who—"

You have no choice. If you allow him to keep it, he will destroy you, me, Lord Callum...and everything we love. You must find a way.

"So what do I do?" I asked miserably.

You are a Shadow. You have the ability to hide, to move about unseen. You must enter the Wizard's domain and take back what is rightfully yours.

I thought about it for a second, then said, "I'll do what I can, as long as you promise to return to the Academy with me afterwards."

I will do what I can to help Lord Drake. But now, we must go. There is no time to waste.

SURPRISE

WITH CAFFALL SOARING in broad circles high above the trees, I made my way in Shadow form toward Marauth's cabin from a Breach that had taken me back to the nearby woods.

My feet left no trace of my presence in the snow, and my breath only puffed out the weakest clouds of vapor in front of my face.

But there was one problem:

I couldn't walk through walls, nor could I open a door in my Shadow form.

I was stuck outside in the bitter cold of the clearing.

Caffall's impatient voice rumbled through my mind as I paused, unsure of how to proceed.

~*What are you waiting for? You must acquire the scepter.*

I can't, I replied, sending my thoughts his way. *I have to wait for him to open the door.*

A coarse growl vibrated its way into my consciousness.

~*No need to wait. I will open the door myself.*

Before I could stop to contemplate what he could possibly mean by that, I saw the dragon fly overhead, shooting into the distance only to bank sharply and head back our way, his entire body glowing like a hot coal.

"Oh, crap," I mumbled, gliding toward the cabin's front door to wait for Marauth's inevitable appearance. Whatever Caffall had planned, it was probably going to involve mayhem of some sort.

An explosion rang through the air. A tree burst into flame some distance away, and then another, and another, until the entire forest seemed to be on fire.

Caffall, it seemed, was going to *smoke* the wizard out of his cabin.

As predicted, Marauth came storming out the front door after a few seconds. He moved more swiftly than I'd ever imagined he could, pulling a long, fur-lined coat around him as he raced into the clearing to see what had happened.

The second he was clear of the door, I slipped inside to tear through the small house in search of the scepter.

I scanned the kitchen, the small living room, the mantel...but there was no sign of it.

Finally, I found myself in a small bedroom at the back of the house, only to see the scepter floating above the bed, rotating slowly as if on display in a museum. I left my Shadow form and reached for the object, only to cry out in pain when a sharp shock shot its way up my arm.

It's being held in place by a spell, I thought, sending the words to Caffall. *I can see it, but I can't touch it. Can you throw another distraction Marauth's way? Maybe it'll be enough to break his hold on the Relic.*

~*Of course.*

Through the window I spotted a sudden flash of orange-red light, then another, and another, as bolts of deadly flame fell from the sky in a torrent of scalding rain.

All around the cabin, the land began to burn.

And as it did so, the scepter fell onto the bed, landing with a soft thud.

I reached for the object, grabbing it and stuffing it through my belt like a sheathed sword, hoping Marauth had fled, terrified, into the woods by now.

I darted toward the front door with every intention of calling on my Shadow form the second I found myself outside in order to avoid the deadly downpour that was still falling from the sky.

But as soon as I was through the door, I came face to face with the fatal flaw in my plan.

Marauth was standing on a patch of damp grass in front of the house, flames rising around him in a hellish display.

Yet he remained unscathed. Untouched.

The white suit that he wore under his coat was pristine.

Damn you, I said under my breath.

Before I had a chance to move, the wizard held up a hand. I found myself lifting off the ground, a series of white ropes coiling around me, pinning my arms firmly to my sides. Far above, I could hear Caffall letting out a cry that sounded too close to defeat for my liking.

I couldn't exactly blame him, though—there was nothing more that he could do. Nothing, at least, that wouldn't kill me as well as the wizard.

"I share the dragon's sentiment, Vega Sloane," Marauth said. "I don't want to end your life. But I can see that you and he have had a productive conversation. I suppose you're displeased to learn about my plan to keep Lord Drake incapacitated."

"You lied to me about the scepter," I replied through gritted teeth as the soles of my feet dropped gently back to the ground. "It's not yours and never was, and I won't let you have it."

Marauth looked genuinely amused, tilting his head to the side. "Won't let me?" he asked. "I must say, it's quite charming how you utter those words as though you have any say in the matter whatsoever."

"I think the burning trees have a say," I told him, my eyes

shifting to the still flaming woods. "You'll die if you stay here. But I can bring you to safety. I can take you through a Breach, if you agree to let me keep the scepter."

This time, the wizard let out a full-on belly laugh.

"Oh, child," he said, turning toward the woods and waving his hand in the air. Instantly, the fire ceased, and the trees, which should have been blackened, were once again covered in a thick coat of fresh snow. "Merriwether hasn't shown you much of himself, has he? A pity that you've been kept in the dark about a wizard's true abilities. I suspect you could have taken after him in so many ways, had you had time to learn. He's an impressive magic user, for all his flaws. He'll be devastated to realize you'll never reach your full potential."

"What are you planning to do to me?" I asked, more angry than frightened.

"For the moment, I intend to keep you here, of course. You're the only thing keeping that dragon friend of yours from burning my cabin to the ground. So come, let's go back inside where it's warm, but not *too* warm…shall we?"

I nodded obediently, even as I tried to come up with a scheme to escape with the scepter still in hand.

"Oh, and before you decide to re-enter the Shadow realm," Marauth added as I turned to head back inside, "I should warn you that the coils around you will allow me to see you, whatever form you're in."

"I wouldn't dream of trying to disappear," I muttered.

When I'd stepped into the small living room, I turned to face him again.

"Tell me, how did you know?" I asked, hoping to stall him for a few minutes before he decided to end my life.

"Know what?"

"That I was in your cabin, taking the scepter while Caffall was burning the woods."

He smiled. "You forget, Vega, that wizards can see a great deal. Past, present, future. We *always* know."

"So you know what's going to happen in approximately thirty seconds, then?"

With that, Marauth's smug grin vanished.

"The dragon will fly off, defeated," he said. "You will hand me the scepter. Then, we shall see."

"*Maybe* those things will happen," I replied with a smirk. I sucked in my cheeks before adding, "Maybe they won't. You know, I'll bet a Witch would be able to tell me exactly what's about to occur. A Witch would know. They're highly intelligent. Probably more intelligent than wizards, really."

"Witches?" the wizard laughed, clearly agitated. "They're lesser beings. Pests on the magical landscape. Mere insects. They know nothing."

"Just humor me," I said. "After all, we're stuck in here together for a little while, aren't we? Can't you just admit that Witches are pretty good at foreseeing future events?"

"Fine." Marauth breathed. "Some Witches can see the future. Others can't. Some dogs can balance a ball on their nose. What of it?"

"See, the thing is, I've been thinking about them a lot lately," I said with a smile. "I met a few of them, you know. I liked them. One in particular. Her name was Solara. She was kind of amazing. I don't know if you've met her. Likes to wear black. Bit of a badass." I let out an exaggerated sigh—or at least as much of one as I could muster with Marauth's restraints still wrapped tightly around me. "I wish she were here. I miss her."

"Yes, well, she's *not* here, is she? So I'd suggest that you shut your mouth, once and for all."

To my surprise, the wizard flicked his hand at me and the conjured ropes finally vanished. I could breathe properly once again.

"Now, let's get this over with. Hand me the scepter," he said, holding out his hand.

I held the Relic out to him, but as I did so, I found myself stepping backwards. To my surprise, the move occurred against my will, as if invisible hands were on my shoulders, urging me away from the wizard.

"Don't play games," Marauth warned. "The scepter. *Now.*"

"I'm…trying," I told him, even as I took another step away from him. "I don't know what's happening to me—it's like someone's forcing me back."

Or possibly pulling me to safety?

My question was answered when a small, spark-like wisp of light moved through the room so fast that I nearly missed it.

WISPS

Wisps of light flitted their way through the cabin. Thin, swirling ribbons of what looked like white smoke, streaking around Marauth, spinning him this way and that as he tried to focus on them—all the while cursing under his breath.

He threw his arms out and shouted a word in a language I didn't understand in a clear attempt to cast a spell.

But the wisps seemed to be immune to his magic. They teased and taunted him, hovering for a second before vanishing, only to reappear a few feet away.

I was sure I heard distant laughter at one point—the amused giggling of women pleased by their handiwork.

And then, a sweet, lulling female voice spun through the air.

"Now, Wizard, you know very well that you can't take all of us on at once. A Witch is, after all, a skilled magic-user…just like you."

"You cannot be here!" Marauth snarled. "This is not your business. Leave me. Leave the girl."

"You're wrong about that."

In an explosion of bright light, Solara appeared in front of the fireplace, crossing her arms and staring the man down.

"The Otherwhere *is* my business," she said. "Perhaps more importantly, the scepter is my business. You know its meaning to me. You know it is not rightfully yours."

"It was given to me *freely*!" Marauth belted like an angry child. "It's mine! A Relic of Power, once handed over by a Seeker, is…"

Seeming to choke on his own words, he stopped talking, backing away as Solara stepped toward him. The powerful wizard now looked like a cornered animal, terrified of what the Witch might do to him. "I have spells at my disposal…" he muttered.

"*You have spells*," she laughed, throwing me a sideways glance just before leaping at Marauth and taking his chin in her hand.

For the first time, I noticed her perfectly sharpened, black-polished nails, which looked like they could easily claw his eyes out. "Yet who is it who now possesses the scepter you claim is yours? A teenager. A girl. Without the power of the Twelve on your side, you are weaker than she is, and you know it. You have broken with your Order. You have betrayed them, the Otherwhere, and every magic user in this land. You know full well that you have no right to the scepter, or even to live."

"It is mine!" he protested again.

But Solara shook her head and clicked her tongue against her teeth.

"Vega Sloane," she said softly, "do you know who crafted the scepter you found in La Baie?"

I tried to speak, but my voice caught in my throat as if a hand was wrapped around my windpipe. Overwhelmed, I set the scepter down on the kitchen table.

"Tell her," Solara said, squeezing Marauth's jaw until he moaned in pain. "Tell her who its rightful owner is."

"She's dead!" he shouted. "She died long ago!"

"Ah, but her bloodline lives on," said Solara, curling her index finger so that the tip of her fingernail dug into his flesh just enough to draw a trickle of blood. "Say her name. Say it."

"Morgana," Marauth whined. "Morgan Le Fay crafted the scepter."

"That's right. My ancestor."

My jaw dropped open. On the first day of our journey, Lachlan had told me about a Coven of Witches whose leader was descended from Morgan Le Fay.

It had never occurred to me that Solara could be that woman —yet it made all the sense in the world.

Solara finally let her hand drop and took a step back. "The scepter, Vega, belongs to my family. To my Coven. It always has. But we allow it to transfer ownership every fifty years, as is the custom for the Relics of Power. We will not, however, allow it to fall into the hands of a devious wizard who would manipulate a Seeker in order to obtain it."

"I did give it to him freely," I said miserably, finally able to speak again. It felt like the most gruesome confession of my life. "I knew who he was. I knew what I was doing. I'm not sure I can take it back."

"Perhaps not. But I can. The wizard used your pain against you—he knew you would surrender the Relic out of love. But that doesn't mean I cannot reclaim it in the name of Morgana."

"You can't! You heard the girl!" Marauth growled.

"I can and will. You have broken an ancient law." Turning my way, she added, "The scepter is powerful, Vega. More powerful than I can say—and you will soon learn what it can do."

"I don't understand…" I said.

"You will. Very soon."

Bursts of light erupted around me, and I turned to see Luna and Merell striding through the room toward Marauth, their lips twitching up in satisfied grins. Together, the three Witches circled the wizard, singing a low chant in some ancient language even as he tried to open his mouth and speak.

But his jaw was locked shut, his eyes white with terror.

Whatever spell he was hoping to cast was stopped in its tracks as the women raised their arms, joining their hands in the air, their chant crescendoing.

Marauth froze for a moment, his mouth suddenly agape as if he was trying to cry out in agony.

And then…he was gone.

"What happened to him?" I asked.

"He has been imprisoned temporarily in a far-off place," Solara said, turning my way. "For breaking ancient laws. For his crimes against magic-users. He will not remain there forever, but until Merriwether and the others of his Order figure out what to do with him."

"It'll be long enough for the bastard to have a think about what he's done," Luna said, crossing her arms over her chest. "The devious old sausage, taking advantage of a young girl like that. Though you should never have given the scepter to him, Vega. You know better, surely."

"Hush," Solara said, holding up a hand. "She had her reasons for handing it over. Love is a powerful force, for any person of any age."

She picked the scepter up and twisted it around in her hands. "A beautiful thing, isn't it?" she asked. "Of course, its true strength lies inside."

With that, she grabbed hold of the silver dragon at its end and twisted until a snapping sound echoed through the small cabin. Horrified, I began to protest, but a moment later, she'd pulled it apart to reveal a small, empty compartment inside.

"The scepter holds a magic deeper than that of any other Relic of Power," she told me. "A magic that has not been used since the days of Morgana."

"What does it do?" I asked, swallowing hard.

"There is an ancient spell, used to bring about what's known as the Melding. The bringing together of two souls that have been Severed."

My heart throbbed in my chest.

Every thread of hope I'd held onto since Callum and Caffall had been torn apart seemed to stitch themselves together inside me.

But I hardly dared to let myself feel the swell of optimism that was working its way into my mind.

"You're saying this scepter can bring Callum and Caffall back together?" I asked, my voice timid.

"It can," she replied. "But the scepter alone isn't enough. There is one element we still need in order to bring the spell to life."

"Tell me what it is," I said, desperate. "I'll do anything, go anywhere."

"You don't need to go far. The material we need is known as *Drakestone*. You've no doubt noticed it already. Red as blood, flowing along the length of the cliff's face."

"The red veins," I replied, nodding. "They're made of stone?"

"They are. We need a piece, and it is best that you, Vega, retrieve it, as you are the one who will cast the spell when you return to the Academy."

"I'm not a Witch," I protested. "I'm no spell-caster."

Solara laughed. "You *are* a spell-caster, as a matter of fact. You turn to mist and disappear. You summon doors, weapons, and creatures. Hell, you summoned us to this place. You may not call yourself a Witch, but you are as powerful as we are. You just haven't quite grasped it yet."

I sat down on one of Marauth's frail chairs, staring at nothing in particular. There was no denying that Solara was right—I had far more in common with her Sisterhood than I'd ever given myself credit for.

"Tell me what to do," I said, pulling my eyes to hers. "And I'll do it."

"Let's go, then," she replied with a grin.

CLIMB

"Seriously? How the hell am I supposed to get up this thing?" I asked as I stared up at the sheer wall of ice and stone some distance from Marauth's cabin.

I looked high into the sky above us to see that Caffall was still circling as though waiting to see what would happen next. I could no longer hear his voice in my mind, but I could feel his presence, like a soothing shawl draped over my shoulders.

"Climb," Solara replied with a warm smile in her voice.

"That's easy for you to say. You can walk on clouds. I'm not quite as gifted as you. I don't have equipment—I'll probably fall to my death or—"

"The closest Drakestone is thirty or so feet up," Solara interrupted. "You will have no difficulty reaching it, Vega."

"You can do that in your sleep!" Luna added in a second attempt at encouragement. "Come on, now. Can't you just summon yourself up there?"

"If there were more than an inch of stone for me to step onto, I could call up a door," I told her. "But as it is, I'd just end up a bloody splatter on the ground in front of you."

"Well, that's not good," Merell said.

"No, it's not," Luna added. "Ah, well, I suppose you'd best get on with it, then."

My teeth chattering, I turned one last time to the three women. "Wish me luck?"

"Luck is for the ill-prepared," Solara replied.

"Break a leg!" Merell offered with a grin, to which Luna responded with an elbow in the ribs. "Hey! What was that about?"

"You don't tell someone who's about to climb a cliff to break her leg. That's a self-fulfilling prophecy if ever there was one."

"Oh. Sorry, I thought I was being nice."

"It's fine," I laughed. "I'll be lucky if a leg is the worst thing I break, honestly."

I stepped forward, my eyes scanning the cliff's surface for any jagged bits of stone to grab onto. I reached up, my fingers finding a small crevice, and hoisted myself a few feet off the ground, only to find a tenuous foothold.

I repeated the motions over and over again until I was too high up—and too terrified—to look down. The whole time, my eyes scanned the barren cliff for the nearest streak of red, but I was quickly beginning to feel like the first set of glowing veins was miles farther away than any of us had thought.

I pulled my eyes down to see that the three Witches had moved back to the tree-line, as though they wanted to stay out of my way in case I really did go crashing down to my untimely demise. They looked so small now. Little black dots in the snow, surrounded by massive, snow-coated pine trees.

My heart hammering, I pulled my eyes back to the cliff in front of me, pressing my forehead to the stone in hopes of catching my breath before daring another look for the precious stone.

Finally, something caught my eye: the smallest hint of glistening blood-red, a few feet up and to my right.

As carefully as I'd ever done anything in my life, I pulled

myself up inch by perilous inch until a fluid line of crimson stone was positioned directly in front of my face.

In a cautious slow-motion movement, I reached for my dagger and pulled it from its sheath with one hand, begging my other hand not to let go of the small bit of rock that was keeping me from tumbling to a hideous fate.

Unsure what to do, I scraped at the red rock, which did little other than result in a little pinkish powder floating away on the breeze. Finally, I pried at a crack in the stone with the dagger's tip, managing to coax out a piece just small enough to fit in my palm.

With all the care in the world, I sheathed my dagger and grabbed the small red stone between frozen fingers, tucking it safely into the pocket of my cloak.

"Now to get back down," I muttered, daring another glance at the earth far below.

I tried to retrace my steps—backwards this time—but quickly discovered that going *down* a cliff with no equipment was even more difficult than scaling it.

Each time I attempted to find a safe haven for my toes, I found myself slipping, letting out shrill shrieks of terror as I did so.

I always managed to re-center myself, but barely.

Below me, I could hear voices hooting and hollering, calling up promises that the Witches had all the faith in the world that I wouldn't go crashing to the ground, and that if I did, I'd probably only break a *few* bones.

It…wasn't helpful.

This game of life or death went on for ten minutes or so before things finally went horribly awry.

I'd found what seemed like the hundredth solid foothold, and put all my weight on the toes of my right foot as I negotiated a new spot for my freezing fingers to grip onto.

But just as I shifted my weight, a perfect storm of terror hit:

the stone beneath my foot cracked and broke free, and my fingers slipped, sending me falling backwards through the cold air, flailing wildly as I reached out to try and grab hold of something.

Anything.

But it was too late.

I was tumbling through the air, my body weightless and excruciatingly heavy all at once.

I wondered in a frenzy of confusion how much time I had before my imminent death.

"Vanish!" I found myself shouting even as I felt my falling body nearing the ground.

My Shadow form came to me just in time to land with all the softness of a feather in the snow below.

I lay there, my eyes closed, unsure whether I was alive or not.

"Vega?"

I looked up to see three faces staring down at me. As I eyed them, each set of lips curved into a relieved smile.

"Neat trick," said Luna. "You really are one of us, aren't you?"

"Thanks," I replied. "I'll take that as a compliment."

"It's the highest form of compliment you could ever hope to receive, in fact."

When I managed to summon the strength, I reached into my cloak, found the red stone, and pulled it out to take a closer look.

It was carved perfectly, like a polished diamond or a ruby. Inside its depths, a swirl of dark red twisted and turned as though the stone itself were a living thing.

As I examined it, the Drakestone seemed to brighten for a moment as if drinking in the meager sunlight. I could *feel* its magic, just as I felt the power of the Relics when they were close at hand.

And for the first time, I knew with utter certainty that Callum would open his eyes again.

FINISHED

"Are you all right?" Solara asked, stepping over to help me to my feet.

I nodded, wiping my hands over my clothing to make sure I hadn't broken anything. "I think I'm okay," I told her. "I wasn't sure I'd survive that."

"We would have seen to it that you did," Luna said. "I was all set to slow your fall, but Solara grabbed my arm, like she knew you'd be perfectly capable of saving yourself."

I smiled at Solara, who nodded, a faint, approving grin on her lips. "You *are* stronger than you think, Vega Sloane. Ending your life isn't quite as easy as you seem to think."

"People keep telling me that," I said. "But I seem really good at coming very close to certain death."

"*Very close* being the operative words. Come, it's time."

"Time for what?"

"For the first step in the Melding."

We walked back to the cabin, where Solara laid the scepter on the rickety kitchen table. As I watched, she called out a word I didn't understand, and the Relic of Power levitated and moved through the air toward me, slowly, carefully, until I was able to reach out and grab it.

"I offer the scepter to you in the name of the Lady Morgana," Solara said in a solemn tone. "It is for you, Vega Sloane, to do with as you will."

"Thanks to you three," I said, looking at the other two Witches. "Thank you for what you did—for coming here. I don't think Marauth was planning to let me live. And I owe Caffall a great deal, of course."

"The dragon is fond of you," Solara said. "He cares about you. You are fortunate—free dragons don't often bond with humans. He must see the same strength in you that I do."

I found myself reddening. How could this woman—this incredible descendant of Morgan Le Fay herself—see me as anything other than a walking disaster? Everything I did involved some kind of mayhem.

Well, *almost* everything.

"The scepter, please," she said, putting me out of my silent misery. "Just for a moment."

I handed it to her without hesitation. She held it, examining the dragon at its head, then grabbed the silver figurine and twisted it.

"The stone," she said quietly.

I pulled the Drakestone out of my pocket and handed it her way. She held it in her palm, whispered an incantation, and the stone turned into a deep red powder. Carefully, Solara poured it from her palm into the small silver compartment and reattached the dragon, which immediately began to glow a faint blue, its eyes turning red.

"The Drakestone's powder is necessary to activate the scepter's spell," Solara said. "Seldom has anyone ever used it for the Melding. Only one time that I can think of."

"Did it...work?" I asked, staring at the dragon, whose eyes

now seemed to glow with the same fire I'd so often seen in Callum's own.

"It did," she said. "Very well. Man and dragon lived separately for many, many years. Rather, they lived lives that were very much intertwined, but their bodies existed as two entirely separate entities. The man was happy for a time, at least. That is, until he disappeared."

Solara's tone had turned sad, as if she spoke of a deeply personal loss.

"You knew the man?" I asked.

"I did...intimately. But our paths forced us apart, and as I understand it, he moved on to a life of solitude. The last time I saw him was nearly seventy years ago."

I wanted to ask more, but something told me I would be overstepping.

"For all I know," Solara finally added, "he's dead by now. He hasn't been seen in decades."

I found myself tilting my head as I looked at Solara. "I'm guessing you're not as young as you look, then."

"No," she replied. "I'm rather old, at least by your standards."

"Skin like a baby's bottom, though," Luna said, beaming with pride. "She hasn't aged a day in five-hundred years, this one."

"Five hundred? Really?"

The revelation made Callum's one-hundred-and-eighteen years seem like nothing.

"Older than that, actually," Solara said. "But those are all stories for another time. Come, let's get you reunited with the golden dragon so you can find your way back to the Academy."

With a nod, I headed for the door, turning back to face the women as I reached it. "There's just one thing—how's Lachlan?" I asked, ashamed not to have inquired about him sooner.

"He's very well. Recovering quickly. At least, his *wounds* are recovering."

I chewed my lip. "You mean..."

"His heart is another matter."

Merell flicked a hand in the air and said, "He'll get over it. He may be gorgeous, but the girl never promised him a damned thing. She doesn't owe him anything. Not so much as a kiss."

"Unrequited love is so cruel," Luna said with a shake of her head. "I remember when I fell for a certain blacksmith in Domburg…"

"A *married* blacksmith," Merell chastised as Solara rolled her eyes at me. Apparently, she wasn't particularly keen on gossip.

"The point is," Merell added, "Lachlan will recover, and when he does, he will be stronger for it."

"Still, I can't help feeling like I've wronged him, somehow," I said, pulling the door open.

"You haven't, child. You've been honest with him. Just give him some space, and you'll find soon enough that he's perfectly content accepting your friendship—even grateful for it. Don't forget, he's been watching you for years. He's become attached, as a wolf becomes attached to its pack. It's a bond that's not easily broken. He simply needs to understand his boundaries. I suspect that Callum's presence alone will be a sufficient reminder of his place in the hierarchy."

I sighed as I stepped into the cold of the outdoors, lifting my face to see Caffall still flying in broad circles overhead as if he was waiting for me.

~Is it time? his booming voice asked.

It is, I replied. *Now it's time to go see Callum. Are you ready?*

~Yes, I suppose I am.

He dove down to land near us in the clearing next to the house. His massive feet hit the ground hard, the snow and ice shooting up in every direction yet managing to avoid the place where we stood. The dragon thrust his head toward us, looking inquisitively at Solara and the other two Witches, though he didn't seem to feel any hostility toward them.

Solara held up a hand, speaking soft words as she stepped

toward the dragon. "You remind me of another," she said, stroking her fingers over Caffall's muzzle. "Like him, you will be happy. You will find peace. Callum will protect you, and you him. But your life will never be what it once was, Drake-kin."

Caffall let out a sound not unlike a purr, and I found myself wondering who Solara was talking about. Who was this other dragon shifter who'd been Severed and then Melded with his inner beast? And why did Solara speak about him in such a wistful tone?

Something told me the Witch wasn't about to share such intimate information with the likes of me, even if I begged her for it.

"You ready?" she asked, turning to me.

"I am."

"You two will fly to the Academy. You will find that Callum is quite well, though still unconscious. But this is the important part. Are you ready?"

I nodded.

"When the time comes to cast the spell, it will come to you. Trust the scepter. More importantly, trust your mind. *Open yourself to the words.*"

I nodded, though I wasn't sure she should put so much faith in my not-so-reliable mind.

"Thank you," I said. "All three of you. For everything. For helping me, and for looking after Lachlan. I don't know how to repay you."

"You are welcome," Solara said. "Come back to us someday, Vega. There's a good deal I'd like to teach you. But perhaps we'll see one another before too long."

"I'd like that," I replied. "And I'd like to send Niala to meet you, too. Or maybe you should go see her. She's staying with…"

"Aithan," Solara said with a nod. "Near La Baie. Yes, we know."

"Of course you do," I laughed.

I stared at Solara for a second before she finally asked, "What's going through your mind?"

"I'm wondering if someday, maybe you could tell me about the...other dragon shifter."

"Someday, Vega the Seeker," Solara said with a melancholy smile. "Perhaps sooner than you expect. But remember that not all love stories have happy endings."

With a bite of my lip and a nod, I turned to Caffall.

You all right with our plan? I asked.

~Do I have a choice?

You're about a hundred times bigger than I am, so I'd say yes.

~Climb on, Vega Sloane. Let's get this ordeal over with.

I pulled myself onto the base of his neck, holding onto his impressive mane of solid gold stalagmites, which seemed to have grown and brightened in the days since he and Callum had been Severed.

The golden crown of spiky scales, which had appeared some time ago on Caffall's head, was more ornate as well.

He looked more than ever like he was meant to be a king of sorts.

Or, at least, a king's most loyal companion.

Waving a final good-bye to the three Witches, I urged Caffall into the air, and he shot like a rocket toward the clouds.

I was at his mercy. The golden dragon could have changed his mind and shaken me off at any moment to soar toward eternal freedom.

Reassuring myself, I leaned forward as he turned toward the Otherwhere's east coast and said, "I *will* give you your Treasure, Caffall. I will give you freedom. I promise."

~I know you will, Seeker.

HOMEWARD

Soaring over the Otherwhere, I pressed myself close to the dragon's neck, daring occasionally to look down at the passing landscape.

La Baie. The Five Sisters. Aradia, hidden away beneath the trees, its Coven of Witches concealed from prying eyes.

A pang of worry struck me as I looked down toward the woods at the base of the mountains. Lachlan had gone from being an enemy to a close friend, and I'd left him with virtual strangers. As difficult as things were between us, the last thing I wanted was for him to be uncomfortable or to feel abandoned.

But I tried to refocus my mind on the east, the Academy, and Callum. It was beyond hard not to let myself grow excited about the prospect of seeing him. Still, I told myself there was no guarantee that he would come back to me. No proof that the scepter I had tucked into my belt would do anything other than look pretty while I waved it fruitlessly in the air.

Apparently Caffall could sense my concern, because his growly voice rumbled through my mind.

You have doubts, Seeker.

"No!" I replied out loud, quickly remembering what a terrible liar I was. "I mean, I don't know. Maybe. I'm hoping for the best, but bracing for the worst."

The worst meaning that Lord Callum remains in a bed for the rest of his—and your—life.

"Yes. For one thing, he hates the thought of being idle for long. For another, he's supposed to do things. Rule the Otherwhere. Be an amazing king. It's a bit hard to do all that if you're lying unconscious in a bed somewhere."

He will rule, Caffall told me. *It is his destiny. It has always been his destiny. I see that now.*

Feeling those words make their way through my mind, my bones, over the surface of my skin—it was as if Caffall had released me from a tension that had inhabited me for months.

Others had told me Callum was meant to be king. But hearing it from Caffall was the only thing that mattered in the world.

"You sound very calm for someone whose life is about to be turned upside down," I said. "You're not scared of what the future might hold for you when I cast the spell—whatever the spell actually is?"

Why should I be scared? If the spell doesn't work, the worst that will happen is that I will remain free. If it does work, I will still remain free. I cannot lose either way.

"I suppose that's true," I said, stroking a hand over his scales. "Tell me, do you know of the other dragon shifter—the one who was Severed from his human side, then Melded with the scepter?"

With that, Caffall seemed to jerk suddenly in the air, like I'd startled him. I grabbed tight hold of his jagged mane and steadied myself as he began to glide smoothly again.

I know of him. He lives in the south, far from the Academy. Far from everything. He used to live among humans, of course. But things went poorly for him.

"Why?"

Because he wanted more than anyone could give him. He was hungry in ways that could not be satisfied.

There was a tone of finality to the dragon's words that told me I'd better stop asking questions.

I supposed I'd never find out who this mysterious Severed dragon shifter was. But whoever he was, I wished him well… assuming he was even alive.

I would have loved to speak to him, if only to find out if the process of Melding was painful for him.

And if it had changed him.

Caffall soared and I reveled in the flight, in the fresh air, in the clouds and landscape beneath us that looked so quiet, so peaceful. Hardly the dangerous terrain I'd crossed days before on horseback.

We began our approach of the Academy after an hour or so, its towers and banners materializing like a mirage in the distance. It looked so quiet, so calm, and a mixture of joy and fear filled me as we began our descent into the eastern courtyard.

I would see Callum soon.

I'd be able to take his hand, to speak to him. To hold him. I would look in his eyes once again.

But I still wasn't entirely certain that I would be able to bring *my* Callum—the same young man that I knew and loved—back to me.

AWAKENING

CAFFALL LANDED GENTLY in the hard-packed dirt of the courtyard, where I was delighted to see that Merriwether was already waiting for us.

He stood to one side, dressed as always in a well-tailored purple velvet jacket and dark gray pants, a smile on his face.

At first I assumed it was me he was happy to see, but when he strode up and lay a hand on Caffall's neck, it became obvious that I wasn't the object of his immediate interest.

"So," he said jovially, patting the dragon as if he was a horse who'd just won a show jumping competition, "she managed to persuade you after all." He turned to me as I leapt down and said, "You have the scepter, of course?"

I pulled it out of my belt and held it out to him. "Here it is," I said, slightly irked. "So, you knew about it? Why didn't you—"

But Merriwether shook his head. "Solara sent a messenger that you were on your way." He studied the scepter for a moment before looking at me and frowning. "I must confess, Vega, that I feel that I've let you down."

"Why?"

"I knew of the scepter, of course—I am intimately familiar with the Relics of Power. But I didn't know about the Melding. The dragon shifter—the one who is now a recluse, who was once Severed from his dragon—his story is from before my time. If I'd known his tale, I could perhaps have given you a little hope."

"I *had* a little hope," I assured him. "Otherwise I wouldn't have gone running off to find Caffall. I just didn't know what I was looking for."

Just then, a set of double-doors behind Merriwether opened, and a bed began to roll itself into the courtyard. No—*roll* was the wrong word, as it had no wheels. No legs, either. Its mattress was simply…floating above the ground.

Under the covers was a brown-haired young man, sound asleep by all appearances.

"Callum!" I cried out, running to his bedside. I pressed my palms to his face, which was cold, though his cheeks, at least, displayed a hint of color.

"What do I do?" I asked, looking toward Merriwether, who was already striding toward us, the scepter in hand. Behind him, Caffall's neck was arched, his head high, bright eyes staring down at Callum.

"You are perfectly capable of casting the Melding spell."

"But I don't know how!" I protested, suddenly convinced that I was woefully unqualified for the job. "What if something goes wrong? What if Callum doesn't wake up?"

"Vega," Merriwether said, stepping toward me and laying a calming hand on each of my shoulders. "You are the granddaughter of a wizard, and of a Witch. You can do this."

"Witch?" I sputtered. "You're saying Nana…my grandmother…is…a Witch?"

"Did you ever doubt what she is?"

At that, I pictured my grandmother in her quaint kitchen in Cornwall, with her mortar and pestle, innumerable potions, balms, and vials.

My brother, Will, and I had always joked as children that she must be a Witch of some sort. But I'd never taken the time to ponder the notion that Witches could even have been a real thing.

"Still," I said, "I'm not sure I know what to do."

"No one wants Callum back more than you do. Which means you are the one who needs to cast the spell. Just trust me on this. I wouldn't lead you astray, granddaughter."

I turned to Caffall, who pressed his face toward us and spoke into my mind once again.

Only this time, I wasn't the only one who heard him.

Vega Sloane has promised me my freedom.

"And you will have it," my grandfather replied. "Callum, too, will enjoy a freedom he hasn't known for some years. And the Time of Dragons will finally be upon us again."

"The Time of Dragons?" I asked. "More than one?"

"There is a war coming, and the Academy—as well as others—will require strong allies. Caffall won't be the only freed dragon you've secured as part of our effort. Are you forgetting Dachmal, and Tefyr, and the others that you rescued from the queen's prison?"

"No, of course not. But I haven't seen them in ages," I said. "I promised them freedom, too. Are you saying I'm going to have to ask them to help us again?"

"I'm saying when the war rumbles toward us like a tidal wave, they will join us in battle. They have work to do yet, and they know it."

I thought for a moment before saying, "You told me a while back that all dragons were once linked to humans. Dachmal and the others—they were Severed from their humans, too, right?"

"They were."

"But they never found their way back together?"

Merriwether shook his head. "No. And their human sides are

long since dead. But the dragons will live on for many years, with our help."

"I'm glad of that, at least. I want the Otherwhere to be a safe haven for them."

"And it will, Vega. But now," Merriwether said, "it's time."

He handed me the scepter and I held it up, unsure what to do.

"Are you ready?" my grandfather asked with a twinkle in his eye.

"Yes, but I..."

"Stand between them, please."

I stepped over, my eyes on Caffall as I positioned myself between him and Callum's bed.

"It's all right," Merriwether assured me. "You won't hurt them. Now, hold the scepter up and close your eyes, then say the words that come to your mind."

I did as he asked, skeptical that it would do any good. No matter what anyone told me, I was no spell-caster. I was still just Vega, the girl who could summon doors and disappear.

I was the girl who liked to flee.

But when I sealed my eyes shut, a series of words snaked their way into my mind, slipping through my thoughts like a length of silken ribbon.

I felt my lips move, and a voice that wasn't entirely my own spoke out loud:

By the light of Morgana's Scepter shall the Two be made whole again.
May they live eternally in peace and prosperity, and may they ever be allies.
Bonded in mind, but liberated in body.

A flash filled the air, and, gasping for breath, I opened my eyes.

"What just happened?" I asked, looking to Merriwether for answers.

"You evolved," he said, gesturing for me to walk over. "As did our two friends."

I looked down at the scepter that was still in my hand, the dragon glowing bright blue once again.

"I have long suspected," Merriwether said, "that you have the makings of what is known as a Sorcière—a Sorceress of the highest order. And the fact that you just performed one of the most powerful spells imaginable proves your strength. Solara and her ancestor, Morgana, are the only spell-casters I can think of with that sort of skill."

"But nothing's happening," I said, dismayed as I looked from Callum to Caffall.

Callum's eyes were still closed, and the dragon looked the same as he had a minute earlier.

"Really?" Merriwether asked. "Perhaps you should look more closely."

I stepped over to Callum's bedside and waited, unblinking, for a sign that the spell had worked.

As I stared at him, his breathing, which had been near-silent and shallow, grew deeper.

And then, like a miracle…he snored.

"Oh, my God," I whispered, my heart on the verge of pounding its way straight out of my chest. "Is he…?"

On hearing my voice, Callum popped his eyes open and he looked up at me. For a second he seemed disoriented, but then he smiled, pulled his arms out from under the covers, and stretched as if he'd just woken up from a nap.

"What time is it?" he asked.

Without answering, I leapt onto the bed, throwing my arms around his neck and squeezing so hard I thought I was going to break him.

He hugged me back, his arms tight around me. "This is nice," he laughed. "But seriously, what happened? Last thing I remember, I…Oh, no."

With that, he pulled himself away and looked around frantically, as if expecting some horrible entity to come flying at him and steal his life away again. He winced, anticipating a strike that never came.

When his eyes landed on Caffall, he tightened, the color vanishing from his face.

"How…" he murmured. "This is impossible…"

"You said his name," I told him. "You said Caffall's name."

For a second, he looked horrified to hear the two syllables from my lips.

I let out a laugh. "It's okay, Callum. We're at the Academy." Twisting around, I smiled at my grandfather. "We're home. You're free. And so is Caffall."

I turned to look up at the dragon, who'd pulled his head away. He was eyeing Callum cautiously, but his golden scales seemed to glow brighter, the crown on his head a little taller than it had been.

"You really are free," I told him. "Just like I promised."

Callum pushed himself up to a sitting position to look at the dragon, and for a moment they seemed entirely locked in a private, silent conversation.

I'd never seen anything so beautiful in my life.

"He's promised to be loyal to the Academy," Callum said after a minute. "He's told me that even though we'll be apart, we will always be bonded. And I believe he's right."

"Are you all right?" I asked, reaching for his arm. "This must be a shock."

"It's like waking up to find that a part of myself has been amputated," he acknowledged. "But something else has grown in its place."

"Really?"

"I don't know how to explain it," he said. "All I can tell you is that I feel more complete than I ever have before…and so does Caffall."

I looked around to see that Merriwether had disappeared.

It was just the golden dragon, Callum, and me in the courtyard.

A trio of lost souls who had somehow found themselves—and each other—once again.

PROPHECIES AND PROMISES KEPT

An hour or so later, Callum, dressed in a gold tunic, black pants and leather boots, was standing in the courtyard to say a temporary goodbye to Caffall.

His hand was on the dragon's neck, and Caffall's sizable chin was pressed to the ground, his gaze focused on Callum.

"I can't believe you're leaving," Callum was saying, his voice breaking slightly. "I can't believe this is possible—us moving apart like this. You've been a part of me for a century, old friend."

He seemed to listen for a few seconds, then said, "I will. Soon. Thank you. And thank you for looking after Vega. For getting her safely back to me."

After another moment of silence, Callum gave the dragon a final stroke of the neck and backed away. He held me as we watched his long-time companion take off for the sky.

"What did he say to you?" I asked. "I mean, if you don't mind telling me."

"He said that I could call on him anytime, just as he might call on me, and we would always be here for one another. But he also said he would be very glad to take you and me somewhere. He feels that we should get used to being together, even if we're apart."

"Take us somewhere? Like on a little adventure?"

"Yes, at some point. To be honest, I'm sort of excited about the prospect of it. I've never actually ridden a dragon. I've only *been* one."

"You're not sad to know you'll never be able to shift again?"

He looked up at the sky, watching Caffall's silhouette disappear slowly into the distance. "I am and I'm not," he said. "We had our share of conflicts, as you know. And I'm glad he's happy. It seems he's found his Treasure at last—it was a need I never fully understood until now. His freedom is the one thing he's always wanted. And you gave it to him. And to me, for that matter. You pulled off a miracle."

I grinned "Don't you see? It's all part of the prophecy. The true heir will destroy the Otherwhere—*unless* he finds his Treasure. When I found him in the Northwest, Caffall was on a tear. He was angry, restless. I don't know what he might've done if we hadn't found the scepter. He might have destroyed the Otherwhere while you slept peacefully."

"It makes sense, I suppose. He's as much the heir to the throne as I am. Separated or not, we're still attached in more than one way. So—you've managed to fulfill an ancient prophecy as well as heal Caffall and me. Is there anything you can't do, Vega Sloane?"

I let out a laugh. "Too many things to count," I replied.

"Well..." he added, pulling me close and kissing me for the first time since I'd lost him, "I'm just grateful you've brought me my own treasure...in the form of a beautiful woman."

"I think being comatose has turned you into even more of a smooth talker, Mr. Drake," I laughed, pressing my palm to his chest. "Come on. Let's get you some food. You must be starving."

"I am, now that you mention it," Callum said. "It sounds ridiculous, but I think sleeping took a lot out of me."

We headed to the Great Hall, which was largely empty. It seemed my fellow Seekers were off doing something more important than stuffing their faces.

"Oh, wow," I said after I'd taken a bite of a warm buttered bun. "I just realized something."

"What?"

"The Scepter of Morgana is the third Relic of Power. There's only the Orb of Kilarin still to find. The other Seekers are probably going to be seriously pissed at me."

"Yeah, they'll be super-angry that you robbed them of the opportunity to almost get killed in some ghastly way," Callum laughed.

"I'm serious. Some of the Seekers haven't had a chance to look for a Relic since the Sword of Viviane. I keep ruining things for them."

"One of them died that night, Vega," Callum said, more serious this time. "By finding the scepter, you really did save them from danger. They should be grateful to you."

"I didn't even know what I was looking for," I said. "It wasn't some noble act of generosity. I was just trying to find my way back to you."

"You traveled across the Otherwhere on horseback. You faced dangerous Waergs. You charmed a Coven of Witches into working with you. All so you could find a way to bring me back to life. I'd say what you did was noble, whether you think so or not."

"Fine, maybe it was a little noble. Still, it was a selfish act. I just wanted you. I wasn't thinking about Relics, or the Academy, or any of it. You're always making me sound so much better than I actually am."

"That's only because you're much better than you think you are." Callum smiled as he ate the last bit of his meal. When he was done, he reached a hand over the table, and I took it. "I know it sounds ridiculous, but I'm exhausted," he said. "Let's find Merriwether and see about some sleeping quarters for us both."

"What? You don't want to crash out in our old tower rooms?"

"I'd prefer something with a larger bed, to be honest."

I grinned from ear to ear at the thought of it. Callum, free of the beast raging inside him.

A private room.

A large, comfortable bed.

It sounded like heaven.

"Oh....crap," I said as we walked toward the Great Hall's doors.

"What's up?"

"Fairhaven," I replied. "My life. School. Liv. All of it. I mean, I know that whenever I step back into my world, it'll probably be like no time has passed. But I'd almost forgotten about that life entirely. Which...seems bad."

"You can go back whenever you like, you know."

"I know, but—wait a minute." I stared at him, nausea threatening to overtake my stomach. "What do you mean, *you*? Are you saying you wouldn't come with me this time?"

Callum's perma-grin faded. "I don't see how I could," he said, stopping in his tracks. "It wouldn't be fair to Caffall. I don't want to separate us in that way, and he can't hide in your world, not anymore. Not like he could before, when he was able to conceal himself inside me."

"But I thought humans couldn't see traces of the Otherwhere. I was under the impression that he was basically invisible to them."

"He is, *basically*. But don't forget, not everyone in your world is human. There are Waergs. Watchers. Spies, agents of the Usurper Queen, of Marauth, of others."

"I hadn't thought of that," I replied, my heart sinking. "So after everything—after every struggle to stay together—I'm still going to have to say goodbye to you. Even sooner than I'd thought."

"It's not goodbye," he protested with a shake of his head. "Not at all. There's still a Relic of Power to find. There's still a queen to defeat. And don't forget your ability to summon doors. There's no reason you can't be here as long as you want, as often as you'd like. I have no intention of saying goodbye to you, Vega, unless that's what you want."

I waited for the usual grim sense of defeat to collide with my mind. The awful panic that set in each time I felt like I was losing Callum.

But this time, it didn't come.

All I could think was, *You lost him—you really lost him—but he's back now. You brought him back.*

And even if you were to lose him forever...

You'd survive.

Because you're strong as hell.

"I suppose you're right," I said. "I guess if you're only a door away at any given moment, it's not like we'd be living a long-distance relationship. But what am I going to tell Liv when you don't come back to Plymouth High? Oh, God. The Charmers will have a field day, thinking you've dumped me and run off with someone else."

"You can just tell them you murdered me in a fit of rage," Callum chuckled.

"That sounds like a great idea. I'm sure no one would arrest me and throw me in prison."

"Not without a body," he replied, tapping his temple with his index finger like he'd just come up with an ingenious plan.

"Clever boy," I said with a laugh as we began walking again. "How about I just tell everyone I'm not that into you and I sent you packing, you know, on account of the fact that you're incredibly handsome, but not quite handsome *enough* for my liking?"

"Sure, but you know no one would believe it. I'm far too charming for you to dump."

"Ouch," I said, sucking air through my teeth, "I'm afraid your charm rating just fell by fifty points, Mr. Drake."

"Damn it!"

"Maybe I could say you were devoured by wolves?" I asked.

"Not a bad idea. As long as I put up a good fight. I wouldn't want anyone thinking I was a wuss."

"I'll tell them you punched three of them in the face before you finally succumbed to your wounds."

"That might be acceptable."

We walked in silence for a minute before Callum said, "There's one wolf I've been wondering about."

"Oh?" I asked, my throat tightening.

"Lachlan went with you on your journey. He looked after you. Is that right?"

"It is," I said. "He protected me more than once."

"Then I owe him my thanks," Callum said, stopping and taking my hand. I twisted toward him and met his gaze. "Just as you owe him yours."

"I am grateful to him," I said. "He knows it...I think."

"I'm sure he does." Callum smiled knowingly. "You know...I have no doubt that many men will fall madly in love with you over the course of your life, Vega. I can't fault Lachlan for being one of them."

I opened my mouth to spew a denial, but nothing came out.

The last time I'd spoken to Lachlan had been tense, not to mention difficult.

I'd told him I could never give him what he wanted.

And hurting him had been one of the most painful things I'd ever had to do.

"He'll be heading back to Fairhaven along with you," Callum said. "We can't both disappear, after all. I want you to know I think highly of him. Don't be too hard on him. Or on yourself."

"Myself?"

"For caring about him."

I pushed myself up onto my toes and gave Callum a kiss. "I do care," I said. "About a lot of people. But I love *you*."

"I know you do. If I'm confident of one truth in the universe, it's that one."

THE ROSE WING

WE HEADED to Merriwether's office, where we found him standing at the far end of the room, perusing his substantial bookshelf.

"How are you feeling, Mr. Drake?" my grandfather asked, turning to look at Callum.

"Not bad," Callum replied. "Although I'll confess I feel like I'm missing something—almost as if I've forgotten some part of myself at home. But I find that when I reach for Caffall with my mind, he's always there...and I'm learning to understand that he always will be." He walked over to Merriwether's desk and picked up a red quill that was sitting on a sheet of paper, twisting it around in his fingers. "As much as I dislike the path that brought me to this place, I do like being here. I feel stronger than ever before, because I don't have to preoccupy myself constantly with my dragon's needs. In a strange way, I think this has made us both stronger."

"I'm very glad to hear it. Not all in your position would have survived the ordeal, you realize."

"I credit you and Niala with my survival. And Vega, of course," he said, turning my way with a smile. "For resurrecting me. I would never have agreed to separate willingly from Caffall, but..."

"But," said Merriwether. "Often when we have no choice in a matter that is terrifying, the answer presents itself. You were willing to die to save Vega and ensure that the Academy got possession of the Lyre. Perhaps this newfound strength is a part of your reward."

"Part?"

"The rest will come," Merriwether said. "Now, you must be looking for accommodations. It's high time the future king of the Otherwhere moved into something a little more elegant than a tower room, don't you think?"

"Let's not get ahead of ourselves," Callum laughed. "I can't become king until I have a plan. And an army." He shot me another glance and said, "And I suspect it would benefit me if the best Seeker in the two worlds found the Orb of Kilarin before I so much as contemplated going to war."

"But no pressure, right?" I asked with a chuckle. "I'm so tired. At least let me have a nap before sending me out there again."

"You can have a very long nap, Vega, my dear," Merriwether said. "The Orb only concealed itself recently. It will be a while yet before it reveals itself to you—or to one of the other Seekers."

I wiped my brow in mock relief.

"Where are the other Seekers—Meg, Olly, Desmond—anyhow?" I asked. "I was expecting to see them when I landed."

"I sent them on patrol. They were going a little stir-crazy around here, so I thought they could use a distraction. In the meantime, *you* need some accommodation. I take it you don't want to head back to Fairhaven just yet?"

"No," I replied. "Not unless you tell me that three weeks have passed there and everyone's frantically searching for my dead body in the woods."

With an impish grin, Merriwether shook his head. "You'll find that mere seconds have passed by the time you return. And when you do...I want you to bring Lachlan with you."

"Of course," I said, shooting Callum a tentative sideways glance. "Liv would go ballistic if he disappeared. But he'll have to get back here first, won't he?"

"Solara will bring him when the time comes," Merriwether said.

"Right. He doesn't have Dudley to carry him. Speaking of the horses, um—"

"Phair and Dudley are happily grazing in a paddock behind the stables. Don't worry." Merriwether headed for the door, opening it. "Come, let me bring you both to a very special wing of the Academy—one seldom seen by its students."

Callum and I threw each other a *Doesn't that sound fancy?* look before following my grandfather out the door and down a series of hallways. After a few minutes, we reached a set of doors that led into the mysterious, hidden wing of the Academy Merriwether had mentioned.

We found ourselves in a broad hallway that was pure white, sculpted out of sleek, polished marble that arched above us in braided tendrils like the branches of a thousand trees.

As we advanced along its length, my grandfather waved his hands in the air. I stopped, bewildered, as the branches surrounding us sprouted a sea of red flowers.

"Roses," I whispered.

"We call this the Rose Wing, in fact," Merriwether said. "As I said, it isn't open to the Academy's students, and few of the faculty even know it's here. It's reserved for the most important of guests."

Through the arched windows to our right, I could see the sea below. The air smelled fresh and clean, and I felt like I'd walked into someone's notion of Heaven.

Merriwether brought us to the end of the hall, where a set of barely visible doors opened to reveal a massive white room, ornamented with Gothic details and intricately carved sculptures of mythological creatures.

At the room's center was an exquisitely comfortable-looking set of furniture—a large white couch with a soft throw blanket. Two oversized armchairs. A floating, stone-surround fireplace that hovered a few feet off the ground, a flame dancing along its insides.

It was magnificent.

"This is known as the Nobles' Suite," my grandfather explained. "There are three bedrooms. You may pick yours."

Callum and I threw each other a self-conscious glance, and Merriwether cleared his throat as if he didn't want to acknowledge the elephant in the room.

Pick…one room?

Or two?

"Anyhow," he said in the most awkward tone I'd ever heard, "I'll leave you to it. When you grow hungry for dinner, Vega, you will know what to do."

Okay, *that* threw me for a loop.

"Excuse me?" I sputtered. "Is there a phone I can use to order room service? Because otherwise, I'm not sure what you're saying."

"You should regard yourself as a *Sorcière* in training now. You are skilled—you always have been—and now it's time to open yourself up to the new world that awaits you. Tap into your mind, and you will find yourself capable of a great deal more than you ever knew."

I shot him a skeptical expression, to which he responded by smirking. "Don't give me that look of yours. The second you set foot in Aradia, you had to know you were among your own kind. The difference between you and them is that you are free to live an independent life outside of the Sisterhood. You are a Worlder, not confined to the Otherwhere or to a Coven."

"I'm open to the idea that I'm the tiniest bit special, I guess," I told him, holding up my hands in surrender. "I just need a period of adjustment. This is a lot to take in."

"Take all the time you need. Now, with that said, I will leave you both. Come see me in the morning, and let me know how you've settled in."

"We will," Callum assured him, guiding him to the door more quickly than was necessarily polite.

When he'd shut the door behind Merriwether, I laughed.

"That was wild," I said, making my way to a corner window to look out at the seemingly infinite horizon. "I'm not sure what to make of any of it."

"Well, like Merriwether said, you have all the time in the world. *We* have all the time in the world, rather." A second later, I felt the familiar, much-craved grip of Callum's arms around my waist. I pressed my head back into his shoulder and sighed.

"It's really going to be okay," I said. "Isn't it? I'm hesitant to say that out loud. But this all feels…right."

"Yes," he replied, "It does."

I turned to him, looked up into his eyes, and I let the tears flow at last.

But for the first time in a long time, they came from a place of pure happiness.

A FINAL PROMISE

AFTER A FEW MINUTES, Callum and I ventured over to a set of doors at the far end of the large living space. Each of us grabbed hold of a handle and pushed, and the doors flew open to reveal a bedroom almost as large as the living room, with a massive king-sized bed sitting against the far wall. The linens were white, as was the marble floor and a layer of thick, furry-looking carpet running the length of the room.

The other furnishings varied between white and the light blue of the sky, and the room exuded comfort and peace.

A set of floor-to-ceiling windows along one wall opened out onto a stone balcony, with an intricately crafted, braided iron table and chairs.

"It seems we've officially graduated to royalty," Callum laughed. "Though I can't say I've done anything to deserve it."

"Me neither," I replied, heading over to the windows to look outside before turning to see that Callum was sitting on the edge of the bed.

"Tired?" I asked.

"I was, but it seems I've gotten a second wind."

I walked over, a nervous lump forming in my throat.

We'd slept together in the same bed many times, of course. But we'd always abided by a strict set of rules.

Kissing was allowed.

Touching was allowed.

Anything further, however, was to be avoided at all costs—as difficult a proposition as it was to restrain ourselves.

The rules had always been in place partially because of the unpredictable dragon who had always occupied part of Callum's body and mind.

But Caffall was gone now. Callum was wholly human.

And right now, I had no idea how that might alter our rules.

"Sit with me for a minute," he said, reading the confusion on my face. "And don't worry."

I did as he asked, and he took my hand in his, stroking my skin gently while directing his eyes to my fingers.

"We're both young," he said.

"I am," I replied. "You're not...at least, not exactly."

"In a way, I am," he said, locking his blue eyes on my own. "Neither of us has much experience romantically—other than with one another, of course. I've changed, Vega. I'm a different person now than I was a few weeks ago. I feel as though I need to learn a thing or two about myself. About you, as well. I'd like for us to get to know each other again."

"I see," I replied, a crooked smile on my lips. What, exactly, was he getting at?

"In less than a year, you'll turn eighteen..."

"True."

"And the thing is, I want to do things the right way. I want our relationship to evolve in a manner that makes sense to both of us."

I turned my head and gave him a puzzled side-eye. "Okay, now you've officially lost me."

He lowered his chin, and I felt my entire body threaten to melt. Callum was so far beyond handsome. A glance from him touched every nerve in my body. A word made me shiver with pleasure.

But this look—this innocent but not-so-innocent expression from a boy who'd lived over a hundred years—it was enough to shatter me in all the best ways.

I was more addicted to him than ever.

"Vega," he said, "you have your own life in Fairhaven. I know that. I know we'll miss each other when you go back. We'll forget each other just a little bit each day that we're apart…but the good news is that we will have many, many reunions." He let out a breath and redirected his gaze to my hand. "The thing is, I want you. I want to find a way to keep you in my life. Not just today or tomorrow, but forever."

A blissful shiver overtook my body.

Forever.

The most incredible word I'd ever heard, from the most incredible person I'd ever met.

"So," he continued, "when you finish high school—when you turn eighteen—"

I shot to my feet and stared at him, cupping a hand over my mouth and shaking my head. "You're not saying what I think you're saying?"

"Depends on what you think I'm saying."

"Callum, be serious."

"I'm saying I want to be bonded with you. For the rest of our lives. Whatever that may mean for us both."

It took every bit of my strength not to crash to the floor. My knees were shaking. My teeth chattered with excitement and confusion. Fear and happiness.

But I didn't say anything.

"Vega? Are you all right?"

"I'm just…processing this," I said. "Processing what you're saying to me."

"I know it's a lot. I know you have college to look forward to, and all sorts of…"

"No," I laughed. "It's not that. It's just…ever since the moment I met you, I've been terrified of losing you." I sat down again, for fear that I really would fall. I stared at my hands, too afraid that if I looked at him, I wouldn't be able to speak. "I have massive abandonment issues, I guess. I'm not sure how to live a life where I'm not afraid you're going to disappear."

"It's not surprising that you have a fear of losing people, after what happened to your parents."

"But I lost you, too, Callum. Days ago. When I saw you lying on the ground in Cornwall, I was sure you were dead. I've never run so fast in my life as I did when I tried to get to you. I thought —seeing you like that—I was going to die. And it scared me. I've always—*always*—told myself to be strong, and independent, and not to rely on anyone, least of all a boy…"

"Ah. So you're saying you'd rather be alone."

"No!" I said, wiping away a tear and finding the courage to look into his eyes once again. "I've had *days* to think about life without you. Days spent traveling, running around, risking my life. It was all to bring you back. If there was the smallest hope, I wanted to make it work. Not because I can't live without you… but because I don't *want* to. It took you nearly dying for me to realize the difference between those two realities. To realize I was strong enough to survive on my own, but that my world is so, so much better with you in it. I realized I could choose my own fate, and the fate I choose is the one with you in it."

Callum stared at me, a funny little smile on his lips. "I'm not quite brave enough to ask what your final answer is, though I…*think* I understand?"

"The answer is that I want to be with you forever, too. Whatever that means. I mean, after I finish high school, of course."

I laughed at the weirdness of those words.

High school.

I'd been through so much. I'd seen friends die, and others fight for their lives and for mine. I'd nearly lost the person I loved most in the world.

But some part of me needed to go back to being an ordinary teenager, even just for a little. I needed to exist in a world where Liv also existed—and where I had a brother. I owed it to Will, after everything he'd done for me—after all the support he'd given me over the years—to finish school.

Besides, I'd need time to come up with an explanation as to why I was constantly disappearing, other than "I'm off to a magical land! See you in a few weeks, or possibly years!"

Callum raked a hand through my mass of dark curls, smiled, and pressed his lips to mine. A kiss filled with joy and pleasure, and all the desire that had built up in both of us over what felt like decades of separation.

I could feel the change in him. The exuberance, the passion. The freedom.

The tension he'd always exhibited—the brute strength required to hold in his dragon—was gone.

But he was still strong.

He was still my Callum.

I kissed him back, releasing the tightness and anxiety that had built up inside my quivering frame. I savored the feeling of his mouth, his lips, the taste of him.

And then his lips were on my cheekbone, my chin, my jaw, my neck. His teeth, scraping along my skin, hungry with a feral energy I was afraid he'd lost when Caffall had left him.

Finally, he pulled back, rose to his feet, and said, "Not now. Not yet. In a year, Vega—when it's official—we will have a night to remember."

With that, he made his way over to the window and plucked at a bit of braided vine that was winding its way down the inner wall of the room. Twisting it in his fingers, he came back to me.

"Hold out your hand," he said, lowering himself in front

of me.

I did as he asked, and he slipped a ring fashioned out of the vine onto my finger.

"It's not a diamond," he said, a slight hint of apology in his voice.

"No," I replied. "It's so much better."

He pressed his forehead to mine and said, "I'm yours, and you're mine. Whatever happens."

"Whatever happens," I echoed. "Only…"

"Uh-oh."

"Well, you know there are complications. You said yourself, you can't live permanently in my world because of Caffall. And if I *leave* that world permanently…"

"You feel like you'll lose your family," he said softly.

I nodded. "When my parents died, I felt a sense of loss that I never wanted to feel again. But that day in Cornwall, I felt it… when I thought you'd died. I can't lose Will…I can't lose Liv. You're my family, but they are, too. Before I can give myself entirely to you, I need to feel complete. Does that make any sense at all?"

"Of course." He puffed out a breath. "How about if we agree to cross that strange, slightly tricky bridge when we come to it? In a year's time, we'll reassess our situation. Until then, we'll simply agree to love one another, whatever that means for us right now."

I smiled. "Deal, Mr. Drake."

We breathed a synchronized sigh of simultaneous deep relief and perfect bliss.

Perhaps I would one day be Callum's wife. Or partner, or whatever I was supposed to call the official nature of our bond.

Titles were of no consequence to me.

The good news was that we would find a way to stay together —a way that didn't involve losing the people closest to me—and the goodbye we'd always feared was no longer a threat.

The bad news, on the other hand, lay just beyond the horizon.

THE BEST SORT OF SURPRISE

THE DAY WAS WARM, and we decided to eat out on the terrace overlooking the sea.

"I've lost all track of time," I said, wandering the living room in hopes of figuring out just how I was supposed to summon a meal. "I don't know if we're about to eat lunch, dinner, or something in between."

"I don't care what we call it, so long as we get to enjoy it together," Callum said cheerfully.

I eyed him, curious to know how long this jovial attitude would last. The Callum I knew had always been wary, on edge, ready for whatever dangerous situation might come his way.

He seemed hopeful now—though I hadn't lost all of my own cynicism.

"We won't be able to enjoy any food unless I figure out how to conjure it," I told him. "I'm beginning to think Merriwether was joking when he said I'd figure out what to do."

I paced the space, my eyes darting everywhere in search of something—anything—that would help to instruct me.

Finally, I spotted a tidily-folded piece of paper sitting on a white bookshelf. I headed over and unfolded it.

"What is it?" Callum asked.

"Not sure," I responded. "It's written in a language I don't know."

"Read it."

I began to form the words.

"Magor...co-meh...kwi...ess," I said slowly, piecing together the syllables as best I could. "Taffle...Kar-nay...veeno?"

Nothing happened.

"Try again. With more conviction this time."

I smirked at Callum, self-conscious. "I feel like I'm taking an enunciation class I never signed up for."

"Just...humor me. Okay?"

"Fine," I sighed, before repeating the words more quickly, my eyes fixed on the table outside. *"Magor come quiesce. Tafel carne vino."*

As I spoke, items began to appear on the small outdoor table.

Plates. A covered dish. Glasses. A bottle of wine.

"Amazing," Callum breathed. "You're summoning food, Vega. Like, food that we can actually eat."

"That's...bizarre," I laughed, leaping out to the terrace to take in the scent.

On the plates were mouth-watering steaks, potatoes, and green beans that looked like they were slathered in butter. When I lifted the lid of a covered silver dish, my eyes met a plate of fresh-baked croissants.

"Let's eat," I said, gesturing to Callum to sit down. "Though I'm not convinced this'll taste like actual food."

Callum cut a piece of steak and popped it in his mouth before scrunching up his features. "Tastes like..." he said.

"What? Tires? A soccer ball? Wood chips?"

"Perfectly cooked steak," he said with a laugh.

"Seriously?"

"Try it for yourself."

I did as he suggested, taking a bite of the most delicious meat I'd ever eaten in my life.

"I don't get it. It can't be real. This can't have appeared out of nowhere."

"Come on—you've summoned far more impressive things in past."

"But I didn't *eat* any of them."

"No—but they were no less real."

"Okay, fine. I'm a badass," I laughed. "I have to wonder what else is up my sleeve."

"Something tells me we'll find out soon enough," Callum said, nodding toward the horizon. I looked out to see a shape gliding toward us, its wings outstretched. They glinted golden in the sunlight.

"Caffall!" I said happily.

"He tells me he'd like to take us somewhere tomorrow, or possibly the next day…before you head back to Fairhaven. Are you game?"

"I am," I replied with a yawn and a stretch, "as long as it's not too early in the morning."

"Of course. We'll sleep in as late as we like. Then we'll see."

"Sounds like heaven."

IN THE MORNING, however, a wrench was thrown into our plans when a knock sounded at the door of the suite.

I wandered over—thankfully dressed—to answer, only to find Merriwether smiling down at me.

"I take it you and Lord Drake slept well?"

I smiled to hear Callum called *Lord*.

"We did," I replied with a stretch. "Is everything all right?"

"Oh, yes. Just fine. Only, I'm wondering if you'd be willing to head to the Grove this morning. Someone is waiting for you there."

I turned to see Callum coming out of the bedroom, a cup of coffee in hand.

"But Callum's *here*," I told Merriwether, confused.

Callum was the only person I'd ever encountered in the the Academy's grove of fruit trees. It was our place—our secret getaway.

"I'm well aware." My grandfather winked, turned away and made his way down the hall. "Any time now, Vega."

"What was that about?" Callum asked.

"No idea. I'm supposed to head to the Grove. Are you okay to wait for me for a few minutes?"

"Of course."

Something told me Callum knew better than I did what was going on. But rather than grill him, I summoned a door decorated with a beautiful orange tree and made my way through, the Breach quickly fizzling away behind me.

When I arrived, I seemed to be standing alone among the familiar rows of exquisite-smelling trees.

"Hello?" I called out. "Is someone here?"

I heard the sound of footsteps landing on fallen twigs, and a few seconds later, Lachlan stepped out in front of me.

Without thinking, I leapt at him and threw my arms around his neck, relieved beyond words to feel him hug me back.

"I had no idea you were here!" I all but wailed as I pulled away, remembering his wounds. "I'm so sorry—did I hurt you?"

"Not even a little." He pulled at his collar to show me there were no signs left of the awful gashes the Waergs had left in his flesh. "I've changed my stance on Witches," he laughed. "Complete one-eighty. They're good people."

"They like you. Especially Solara."

"I like her. She's exceptionally kind. And empathetic. She reminds me of someone I know pretty well."

I found myself reddening, but for once, I wasn't irritated with Lachlan for flattering me.

"Listen, Vega," he said, "I know we'll be heading back to Fairhaven sometime. I just…I wanted to say I'll always watch out for you. But I'll keep my distance, too. But I can't promise I'll leave you alone if I'm worried about you. It's too hard for me. But I'm sorry for the things I said. I'm sorry I put you in that position."

"I know." I hesitated for a second before I told him, "I don't *want* you to leave me completely alone. I never did. I just…I felt torn, you know?"

"I know. And it wasn't fair of me. It was selfish. Everything I've done…everything I've said. I've put you in the most awkward positions."

"It's all right," I told him. "You did what you needed to. Though I'm still not convinced you really *had* to kiss me that night in Volkston…"

"We'll never know, will we?" he asked, a crooked grin on his lips. "Oh, God. Callum must hate me."

"Actually, he doesn't," I said. "He's grateful to you. He's not exactly the most insecure man in the world. I think he knows how much…"

"He knows how much you love him," Lachlan said with a nod.

I bit my lip and nodded back, thinking about what Solara had said to me about loving more than one person.

The truth was, I did love Lachlan. Just as I loved Will, or Liv. He was my family. My friend. He was a part of me.

But I couldn't say the words to him. Not just yet.

Instead, I simply hugged him again and asked, "Do you want to go get a bite? We can grab Callum and head to the Great Hall… if that's okay with you."

Lachlan grinned, and for the first time since I'd met him, I knew he was genuinely happy.

"I'd love that," he said.

EPILOGUE

LACHLAN and I were sitting in the Great Hall with Callum, enjoying a quick bite of breakfast, when the doors swung open and a large party came striding in.

I nearly choked when I saw them.

Solara was at their head, dressed as always in black, and to her right and left were Aithan and Niala.

But behind them were Desmond, Oleana, and Meg, as well as what looked like the Academy's Rangers, dressed in dark crimson.

Callum, Lachlan and I rose to our feet to greet them. The Seekers and Niala had to take turns throwing their arms around Callum and expressing to him how glad they were to see him standing on two feet.

"We were sure you were a zombie!" Desmond told him. "Just a shell of a man. Useless, really."

"Des!" Olly chastised. "What the hell?"

"You have to admit, he was looking a little undead."

Meg smacked him upside the head, and I found myself snort-laughing.

"Glad to see you two have met," I told Solara, gesturing to Niala, who was talking to Callum.

"Yes, we have. She's gifted, as you said. And a quick learner. I've invited her to Aradia to apprentice with us."

"That's amazing!" I replied. "I'm sure she's thrilled."

"Yes, she seems to be. For more reasons than just one," Solara said, nodding toward Aithan, who was staring lovingly at Niala. It seemed I wasn't the only person whose love life was on a positive trajectory.

"Listen, it's not all good news," Solara said, waving a hand to draw the attention of the others. "In gathering your friends, I was given some disturbing information. Come, let's sit and talk."

"What is it?" Callum asked, his mood altering from jovial to business-like in a flash.

"Aithan?" Solara said. "Perhaps you should fill our friends in."

The Ranger cleared his throat. "We met up with a number of Rangers coming up from the South," he said. "They'd been near Kaer Uther. They tell us the Usurper Queen's armies are recruiting Ursals—the large fighting bears from the depths of the south-eastern lands. They're herding them to Uldrach for training."

"It will take some time for them to train Ursals," Lachlan interjected. "They're wilful, not easily tamed."

"True," Solara said. "It will take time. But there is another piece of news—one that I bring reluctantly."

"What is it?" I asked.

Solara looked me in eye. "I told you the Scepter of Morgana was once used on another man," she said, eyeing Callum for a moment. "A man who had a bond with his dragon, like Lord Drake does with Caffall."

"You said you thought that man might be dead," I replied.

"For many years, that was my assumption. But last night, in a vision…"

"Yes?"

"I saw a dragon soaring through the sky toward me from beyond the Chasm."

"Chasm?" I asked. "Where's that?"

"It's a massive canyon in the south of the Otherwhere," Callum explained. "It cuts east-west, and nothing can cross it. At least, not on foot. The lands beyond it are largely devoid of life—or so we thought."

"Correct," Solara confirmed. "All that lives beyond it is forsaken. But I saw the dragon...and on his back was the man I'd once known. He was very much alive."

"I don't understand," I said. "You mean the dragon shifter who was Severed? Isn't that good news? It sounds like you two were close once."

"We were," she replied. "Very close. But his ambition tore him—and us—apart. There was a time when it nearly destroyed the Otherwhere."

She eyed Callum again, and I turned to him, confused.

The color had drained from his face, and he looked as if he understood some deeper meaning behind her words.

"What is it?" I asked. "Why do you two look so freaked out?"

"Because the man on that dragon's back...he isn't just some random dragon shifter," Callum replied with a grimace. "And if he's who I think he is...I may have a challenger when it comes time to take the throne."

"Who...exactly...do you think he is?" I asked, pulling my eyes to Solara's. "What's his name?"

"His name is Meligant," she said. "He is the brother of the man who was once known as the Crimson King."

~End of Book Four, Seeker's Promise~

COMING SOON: SEEKER'S HUNT

War is coming to the Otherwhere, and the last Relic of Power is still hidden somewhere, awaiting its Seeker.

In the meantime, Vega has returned to Fairhaven, where things appear to have gone back to normal...at least for now. But a new threat has risen in the Otherwhere's South, and there is little time left to make the ancient prophecy come true.

Betrayal, bonds, and a battle in Fairhaven will threaten Vega's life, her love, and the family she's managed to build against all odds.

Will she be enough to stop the danger in its tracks?

Seeker's Hunt is available for pre-order, coming in February 2021.

ALSO BY K. A. RILEY

Seeker's World Series

Seeker's World

Seeker's Quest

Seeker's Fate

Seeker's Promise

Seeker's Hunt

Seeker's Prophecy

Resistance Trilogy

Recruitment

Render

Rebellion

Emergents Trilogy

Survival

Sacrifice

Synthesis

Transcendent Trilogy

Travelers

Transfigured

Terminus

Academy of the Apocalypse Series

Emergents Academy

Athena's Law Series

Book One: *Rise of the Inciters*
Book Two: *Into an Unholy Land*
Book Three: *No Man's Land*

ABOUT THE AUTHOR

If you're enjoying K. A. Riley's books, please consider leaving a review on Amazon or Goodreads to let your fellow book- overs know about it.

And be sure to sign up for the newsletter at www.karileywrites.org for news, book-related giveaways, quizzes, contests, behind-the-scenes peeks into the writing process, and advance information about upcoming projects!

facebook.com/karileywrites
instagram.com/karileywrites

Printed in Great Britain
by Amazon